The Accidental Adventures of Doreen Sizemore

SERENA B. MILLER

LJ EMORY
PUBLISHING

LJ EMORY PUBLISHING

Find more books by Serena B. Miller at *SerenaBMiller.com*
Find her on Facebook, *FB.com/AuthorSerenaMiller*
Follow her on Twitter, *@SerenaBMiller*

First L. J. Emory Publishing trade paperback edition February 2016

For information about special discounts for bulk purchases, please contact L. J. Emory Publishing, sales@ljemorypublishing.com

Cover and interior designed by CJ Technics

Printed in the United States of America
10 9 8 7 6 5 4 3 2 1

ISBN 978-1-940283-20-3
ISBN 978-1-940283-21-0 (ebook)

Author's Note

I have long wondered if a train might be an ideal place to write, so I finally took a trip on one. The destination was my sister's place in Arkansas. I had big plans to get a lot of work done on my next novel while traveling along but then a friend texted me and suggested I write a story about riding the Texas Eagle instead.

It doesn't take a whole lot to distract me, so as the train ate up the miles to Little Rock I pulled out a fresh notebook and began describing what I saw around me. The newborn triplets riding alone on the train with their mother, my tattooed seat-mate, the guy with dreadlocks who cursed at everything that woke him up.

As I wrote, the voice of an old Kentucky woman began to develop. She had lived a hard-scrabble life and had the no-nonsense voice of many of the elderly Appalachian women I had known as a child. To my amusement, she was quite opinionated and had a lot to say about things. I threw in a rather ridiculous murder and seven hundred miles later the story was finished and I could hardly believe how much I had enjoyed myself in the writing of it.

This was an important discovery because most writers were once little kids who just liked to tell themselves stories. Then we grew up and some of the joy of telling stories got lost in working out business contracts, meeting deadlines, worrying about sales, and satisfying editors who were often even pickier than my high school English teacher.

I've written several Doreen adventures since then, and like the one I wrote while on the Texas Eagle, each one has been based on a small adventure of my own and each one has been enormous fun to write. Many of my friends and readers have asked for a paperback collection of them and I'm happy to oblige.

I hope you have fun accompanying Doreen on her accidental adventures because I certainly have enjoyed writing them.

Murder on the Texas Eagle

Frankly, if it hadn't been for my baby brother, Ralph, doing the asking, I never would have went on this trip. Even now, sitting here in my Amtrak "roomette" watching the state of Texas fly by, I'm coming real close to regretting the family loyalty that made me step foot onto this train. I'm already as tired as sin, and there's still a lot of miles to go before my brother picks me up in San Antonio.

"Why don't you hop on a plane and come down for a nice, long visit," Ralph had said, off-handed-like, during our once-a-month phone visit. He acted as though traveling so far wouldn't be no trouble to me at all. "I'll pay for your ticket."

I held the phone away from my ear and gave it a good, hard look. Was this man serious?

"I'm seventy-one years old, Ralphie. I don't just 'hop' anywhere anymore."

It made me feel good that he wanted me to come bad enough to pay for my ticket, but it weren't no hop-skip-and-a-jump from South Shore, Kentucky, to the state of Texas. It ain't that easy for someone like me to claw my way out of the hills of Kentucky. I ain't been more than fifty miles away from home in sixty years, and he wanted me to just grab a plane and fly to San Antonio? My brother didn't realize how much prayer and planning and hard thought I'd have to put into such a thing.

Texas has always felt like it was on the other side of the world to me, especially since Ralph and his wife, Carla, went there on a vacation and decided they weren't never moving back home. It like to broke mama's heart and mine, too, truth be told.

"If it's all that easy, how come you ain't done it yourself since Aunt Edith's funeral six years ago?" I asked. "The plane flies both ways, you know."

"I've been busy, Doreen." His voice took on that pouty sound he used to have when he was a boy and I'd smack his dirty little hand for sticking it in the cookie jar right before dinner. I could almost see his lower lip poking out, even if he is in his sixties. Mama spoiled my baby brother rotten when he was little and him getting older don't seem to have taken one bit of the spoiled out.

I was working up a huff over that "busy" comment when he said the words that shut my smart mouth right up and rocked me back on my heels.

"Carla's sick, Doreen. Real sick. She has to have chemo. I need somebody to help me take care of her so I can keep working."

"Oh, Ralphie," I felt sick at heart. "I am so sorry."

Carla is a sweet girl. I've always liked her and I was real sorry I'd snapped at him like that.

"I need you, Doreen," he pleaded. "You gotta come help me. I don't have anybody else to turn to."

"Let me think on it," I said. "I'll call you back tomorrow."

I hung up the phone wondering what in the world I was going to do. I didn't want to let my brother and sister-in-law down, but I couldn't hardly face going all the way to San Antonio, neither.

Our home town of South Shore, Kentucky is good enough for me. Always has been. Always will be. I don't understand why people feel the need to move far, far away. We've got that pretty Ohio River and all them beautiful hills to look at. I figure if you can't find what you're looking for in South Shore, or across the bridge in Portsmouth, or just down the river in Ashland or Ironton—you don't need it.

It's my brother who left and went far, far away. Ralph and me never did see eye to eye about the need for him to stay here where he belongs. Carla was never any help at keeping him home, neither. She's a local girl, but she's one of them women who do whatever her husband tells her to. If Ralphie told her he wanted to go live on the moon, she'd go to Goodwill and start looking for a moon suit. San Antonio seems like such a strange place for a Kentucky boy, born and raised, to end up but there's something about it that caught Ralph's attention twenty years ago and just never let go.

I'm not afraid of flying. Not that I've ever flown, but I'm not afraid of the principle of it. The way I figure it is if a person has lived right with the Lord, and is on the other side of seventy, there are worse ways to go than a plane crash. Like Vera Adkins. After that stroke she's lingered for years now not able to speak one word unless it is a cuss word. I'm telling you the God's honest truth. And her a good church-going woman who never said a bad word in her life. Sometimes I suspect that she might have said a few in her head through the years, though, for 'em to be in there.

Vera still comes to church, of course, but we try not to let her get too excited or try to testify for fear that she'll attempt to say something like "Praise the Lord" and something else entirely will shoot out of her mouth. Her daughter took her to a church pot luck last month and when Vera forgot herself and tried to say "Please pass the salt" a string of bad words came out of her mouth and the pastor was sitting right across from her. It was funny in a way, but we all tried real hard not to laugh.

I forgot my train of thought. Now, what was it I getting ready to say?

Oh yes, big airports and how we ain't got any around here.

One of the few bad things about living in South Shore, Kentucky is that all the nearest airports are at least two hours away. Columbus, Cincinnati, Lexington. There's just no easy way to get to a plane from here. To fly, I'd have to ask my neighbor, Bobby Joe to drive me there. I don't like having to ask someone who ain't close kin for favors and everyone who was ever close kin has moved away now that most of the factories have closed up around here. Bobby Joe is a second cousin, though, and he helps me out from time to time. His new little wife, Esther, is a sweet girl and I'm grateful to have them living next door to me.

Problem is, even though I'm not afraid of crashing in an airplane, I am afraid of trying to find my way around an airport even if Bobby Joe didn't mind driving me all the way there and dumping me off at one. I've seen them airports on the television set and I can just picture myself wandering around, lost and old, carrying that suitcase my mama bought for me to go to New York City that time we took our senior class trip way back in high school. I'd probably end up missing my plane and then where would I be?

As far as I was concerned, Doreen Sizemore had no business wandering around an airport unless someone smarter than her took her by the hand and led her like a little child. I hate to say it, but it's true. This is one old woman who knows her limitations.

Not that I can't get around. I do all right. I'm not on a walker or cane or anything. I still got me a big ole garden and I take care of it all by my lonesome. My people never did run to fat like some folks do, so that helps, too.

I even killed me a big rattler that hid out in my garden last summer. I was still nimble enough to jump back out of the way when it tried to bite me. Of course, I'm scared enough of snakes that I'd a probably jumped out of the way even if I was as old as Methuselah. I killed that old meanie with a sharp garden hoe. Chopped him up into a million little pieces 'cause I was so scared. Frank Fuller, over at church told me I'd wasted some good meat. He said rattlesnake was tasty. I can't imagine eating snake. I hate them things. Just hate 'em.

Shoot. I lost my train of thought again. What was I saying?

If I remember right, it didn't have nothing to do at all with snakes. Oh yes. I was talking about Ralph wanting me to come out to San Antonio and help him take care of his wife who got cancer. No doubt she's as scared of that disease as I was at finding that rattler in my beans—except there's no hoe big enough to help her with that.

I seen a lot in my life. Carla might make it through. She might not. But I figure she might feel a mite better with Doreen's homemade chicken noodle soup in her belly while she's fighting it.

There's no getting over the fact that I'm worried sick about her. I know I'd worry less if I could take charge of her kitchen while she goes through chemo. Mama got all picky about her food, like most people do who go through that. I'm no nurse, but I've learned a few things about caring for sick people during bad times.

Ralph's not going to be any help to her, that's for sure. I know my brother. The last I checked, he barely knows how to use a can opener to feed himself—let alone deal with the kind of tiny bird-like appetite Carla is going to have.

I was going somewhere with this. I know I was, but this news about Carla has me so shook up I hardly know which end is up.

Oh yes, I was talking about trying to get there.

Bobby Joe's truck has been acting up, plus he's been a tad grouchy ever since he got into that fuss with his foreman over at the OSCO stove company and lost a perfectly good-paying job which don't come easy around these parts let me tell you!

Then Esther had little Maggie. She's only four weeks old and a more colicky child I never did see. Ever since that baby was born, if I started getting blue and lonely, I would just trot over there and spell Esther by walking that fussy baby up and down her living room floor and then I'd feel a little bit better. Besides being a fussy baby, Maggie looks just like her mama... poor little thing. Esther's got a sweet disposition, but she's no looker.

Anyway, Esther and Bobby Joe don't seem to mind taking me to the grocery store or doctor visit from time to time, but I didn't think it would be a good idea to ask either of them to drive me all the way to Columbus. Weren't sure Bobby Joe's truck would make it.

It ain't that I can't drive—I can. It's just that I've been having a few dizzy spells here lately, and its one thing to accidentally kill myself in a car wreck. I'd be willing to take that risk to keep my independence. But it's a whole other thing to accidentally take someone else's life. What if I was to plow into a young family? I'd never forgive myself, and I don't think the Almighty would be none too happy with me, neither. So I sold my old car a couple years back and put that money in a little account that I'm intending to give to Bobby Joe—except he don't know about it and I thought I'd make him work for it a bit while I'm still around. Won't hurt him none. Bobby Joe is a little on the lazy side.

I can talk about him. I got the right. He's kin. Not saying anything that ain't true.

It would be nice if I had someone to drive me to Texas, but I don't. Even if Bobby Joe's truck was working good I wouldn't ask him to drive me that far. The way he's been acting since that colicky baby showed up, I'm not sure he'd come back. He's not been known for sticking to things. Bobby Joe is a good boy, but he likes life to be easy. He ain't lived long enough to figure out that easy ain't always best.

I worried at the problem all day like an old dog with a bone and no teeth. That night I lay in bed puzzling over what I was going to do. I prayed a good bit too. Figured it would be good idea to talk to Someone a whole lot smarter than me about the problem.

The toughest thing about getting old ain't so much the aches and pains. The toughest thing is that you lose so many people. All the one's you was friends with back when you were young are either sick and all crippled-up or dying off. The only thing good about growing old is that you tend to grow closer to the Lord if you're a mind to. You kinda have to. You run out of people to sop up all your time and after while it's just pretty much you and God and the telephone that don't ring all that much.

Tonight, though, God was being awful silent and I just couldn't get any peace at all.

It was in the middle of the night and I was tossing and turning and flipping my pillow every which way trying to get comfortable when I heard the clackety—clack of the train behind my house. I'm so used to it I don't hardly pay any attention to the sound anymore. It's kind of like my Mama's old regulator clock that I stopped hearing go tick-tock about seventy years ago.

My nerves was in such a state, though, the sound of that train seemed to shake the house like it was going to run right through my kitchen. It was then that a new thought hit me like a ton of bricks. I could take a train to San Antonio. It might take a whole lot longer than a plane, but I didn't have nothing else I had to do.

You might think it strange that it didn't occur to me earlier to take the train, but people in South Shore just don't do things like that very often. For one thing, it ain't all that handy. Number 51 Cardinal passenger train only chugged through town three times a week in the middle of the night. Sometimes I might be awake at eleven o'clock or so when it was due—it never was too reliable—and it would stop to pick up or drop off a passenger, but it didn't happen a lot.

I knew that it went through Cincinnati and on to Chicago where a person could climb on trains going all over the nation. I didn't know what the name of the train was that went to Texas, but I was pretty sure it was possible to get one that went close enough to Ralph in Texas that he could come pick me up.

There weren't no real train depot in South Shore. Don't think for a minute there was. All we had was a boxy little building on the corner of Main Street and Route 23 with plastic windows that was kept lit up at night. The only thing in it was a long, blue bench with plenty of graffiti carved in it and a heater if you was lucky. There was never any to-do made about our train station. The train just kind of sneaked up when nobody was looking and from time to time it whisked somebody off. Mostly we just forgot it was there.

The amazing thing was—that little plastic train-stop building was only a half-mile from my house and I could walk to it—even carrying my old suitcase. If I could figure out how to take that train, I wouldn't have to ask no one for a ride or nothing!

I lay there all excited at the thought of the freedom of it. For a couple of seconds I felt almost giddy with the idea of the adventure. Just walking to the train stop, getting on, and going where I wanted. Then reality started to creep in. I was seventy-one years old and sometimes I do get these dizzy spells.

So I went from being giddy at the thought, to being scared again. Who was I kidding? I was too old to do this. Wasn't I? I didn't even know how to buy a ticket. There weren't no ticket agents in that little-bitty train passenger box. I'd be lucky if it had all its light bulbs screwed into the sockets. There's been an awful lot of thieving going on around here since some of our local boys started taking that ole meth. I've heard some of 'em are foolish enough to try cooking it, too. There was an explosion not too far from here that made the papers.

Now I'm off the subject again. I'll try real hard not to do that.

So I laid there thinking how scared I was. Then I got to thinking about Carla again, and how scared she must be with what she's facing. I got upset all over again because I knew for sure that I was gonna try to ride that dang train whether I wanted to or not 'cause that's the kind of person I am where family is concerned. If they need me, I'm going to try to find a way to help them. Then I got mad all over again at Ralph for choosing to live so far away that he went and put me in the middle of this mess.

It was a rough night.

When the light of dawn finally cracked through my window blinds, I gave up and got out of bed. First thing I did was feed the old tomcat that's usually hanging around my house in the morning. He's a tough one, that cat is, and suspicious. My lands! That cat is surely careful not to get too close to folks. It's been three months I've been feeding him and he just yesterday let me pet his head real careful with only one finger. He kind of closed one eye and squinted up at me like he couldn't believe I'd be foolish enough to try, but he didn't bite my hand off so I think we're making progress. Then I boiled some water, made me some Sanka, put enough sugar and evaporated milk in it to cut the bitterness, and worked up the nerve to call Ralph and tell him about my idea of riding the rails to Texas.

I rolled that phrase around in my mouth a minute, liking the sound of it. "Riding the rails."

"Doreen," I said to myself. "If you can cut a three foot rattlesnake to smithereens with a garden hoe, you can manage to go ride on a train for a couple of days to help your little baby brother in his hour of need."

My brother, Ralph, is not exactly a little boy anymore though. We run to big-boned in my family and he's a six footer with a solid three hundred pounds on his frame, but whenever I think about him, I always see that little fellow what used to crawl into bed and cuddle up with me whenever the thunder and lightning started and he got scared.

I dialed the number. He picked it up on the first ring like he'd been sitting there worrying about what I was going to decide. The minute I told him what I was thinking, he got all excited and said he'd pay for it. I told him my money was as good as his if I could just figure out how to get a ticket. He said not to worry about a thing, that he'd take care of everything. He called back later and told me he got a good deal so that was all right. He explained the details to me and then we hung up.

I figured there was no turning back now. I was grateful when I looked up at the clock and saw it was just about time to leave for my appointment at Betsey's Beauty Boutique. With me getting ready to go to Texas, if I ever needed me a good perm, it was now. I walked on over, thinking it might be a long time before I ever saw Betsey's Beauty Boutique again.

The girl who usually does my hair is Holly, a sweet girl with a pretty face. She always gives me an extra-curly perm because I like to get as much value for my money as possible. For the life of me, I do not know why the girl thinks a nose ring is attractive but maybe it's a phase she'll grow out of someday, poor thing.

I told her all about my new adventure, and I told her I was thinking about getting Bobby Joe to take me across the bridge to the Big Lots store in Portsmouth so I could buy one of them suitcases on rollers I seen there. I'd been studying on things and I wasn't sure I was still strong enough to tote around the suitcase I carried on my class trip to New York City. It ain't like I'm eighteen anymore.

"I tell you what, sweetie," she said. "Don't go and do that. I got a suitcase you can borrow."

She's like that, Holly is. She calls people sweetie and honey and baby doll and don't even realize she's doing it half the time. Just trying to make them feel good, I guess, and truth be told, most of us can use a little perking up. The girl's got a big heart. She's Elmer Stoker's granddaughter and I think she must get some of that sweetness from him. I always liked Elmer when we were kids. He was a kind child. I surely did hate it when he got that Leona Beardsley in the family way and had to marry her. Poor man has been hen-pecked half to death ever since.

I suppose some people might say that it served him right, but Leona has the sourest temperament I never did see. Humiliates Elmer even in Sunday morning Bible class, harrumphing and rolling her eyes if the poor man makes the slightest remark. So help me, I think if Elmer said for God so loved the world that he gave his only begotten son that whosoever believeth in him

20 SERENA B. MILLER

should not perish but have eternal life.....I think Leona would find fault.

Thank goodness Elmer's granddaughter took after him in the personality department. If she took after Leona, I'd have to find me somebody else to give me my perms.

"I'll tell you what, baby doll," Elmer's granddaughter said. "I got me the prettiest roller suitcase the other day. It was on sale and I couldn't pass it up. I'm not going anywhere for a good while, so you're welcome to take it on your trip."

I hated taking her pretty suitcase away from the girl. I ask her where the good deal was.

"Oh," she said, like it was the most natural thing in the world. "I got it on Amazon."

For a minute, I wondered if the ammonia in my perm was addling my brain. I didn't remember hearing anything about that girl going to the Amazon. News like that would get around. People in these parts don't just get up one day and prance off to the Amazon.

"Why on earth would you want to go there?" I asked. "I heard they got awful big snakes in that river. The kind that can swallow you whole."

Well, Holly just about wet herself laughing over that. Doubled over, she did. Then she had to tell the other two girls what I said. I sat there with half my hair up in perm rollers feeling stupid. Then, after she caught her breath, she let me in on the joke and explained which Amazon she meant and she wasn't talking about no river.

Sometimes I feel like I'm living in a different world than everyone else these days. My cold feet over getting on the train suddenly got worse because I had misunderstood about the Amazon. What other things might I misunderstand? I felt a panic setting in.

"Maybe I shouldn't go after all," I said. "Maybe I'm too old."

"Don't be silly." She tapped me on the shoulder with a comb. "My boyfriend rode that train to Chicago and then onto Oregon and back again when he was out there looking for work. He said it was a cinch."

The girl could not have said any words that would've made me feel any better. I happen to know her boyfriend very well and that child really did get the short end of the stick when it came to smarts. He didn't even know enough to blow his own nose when he was a kid. He'd just stand there looking at you like he didn't see anything wrong with having all that stuff hanging down over his upper lip. I always kept a box of tissues in my Sunday school class, knowing that he would need a good wipe and blow before the class was over.

He turned into a right handsome boy after he got done growing up and I think he finally figured out how use a handkerchief, but it still kinda gags me to remember what he looked like when he was seven. Poor thing.

Now, I figure if that boy has enough smarts to figure out how to travel by train, it's something I should be able to manage.

Holly brought me her little wheeled suitcase later that night after she got off of work. Brought it right to my door. That's the way things are in a small town.

It was red and had a lot of zippers. I wondered what I was supposed to put in all them zippered pockets.

"Now, you take care, Miss Doreen." Holly gave a little wave after she'd sashayed back to her truck. Hers had a gun rack in it. I thought it was probably her daddy's but you never know around here. Sometimes our women folk drive around with their own guns and gun racks in their trucks. Kentucky women ain't never been shy when it comes to guns, except maybe the ones who live in the big cities and don't know no better.

The next day, I gave Esther next door all my cat food so she could take care of my stray tomcat. She had seen the scars on that old tomcat and the bit-off ear and she looked doubtful. I told her he wouldn't hurt her if she didn't hurt him. I could hear the baby crying in the living room and Bobby Joe a'trying to sing it to sleep. That surprised me and I gave Bobby Joe points. He might grow up to be a decent father after all.

I walked down to the bank and paid all my utilities for the next two months. No telling how long I might have to be there, but paying that far ahead took about everything I had. Then I ironed and folded five housedresses and a couple of slips into the suitcase plus one good dress for church. I put enough unmentionables in there to get me through a week and some ankle socks. It was funny how shabby everything looked inside of that new, pretty suitcase but I couldn't help that.

I used the zippered pockets to store my plastic pink rollers, some Pepto-Bismol tablets, some Vicks Vapor Rub, a toothbrush and my extra eye glasses. I've never been a person who wore a lot of makeup, but just in case, I stuck in a tube of Red Sin I'd bought one day when I lost my mind in the Dollar Store and thought I might try to fancy myself up a little bit. Thoughts like that come over me from time to time and usually I ward them off, but that unused tube had been sitting there on my bureau for a couple years without me figuring out a good time to wear it so I figured maybe it would be a good item to put in one of them little zippered pockets. I've heard Texas women are kind of fancy.

Then I made me some peanut butter sandwiches, put some carrots and celery in a bag, and put a whole new package of Juicy Fruit in there, found my Bible and handkerchief, stuck everything in my biggest purse and figured I was as ready as I was ever gonna get.

I watched the television set until long past my normal bed time of nine o'clock. I watched until ten o'clock. The time had come to turn off the lights, lock the doors and start walking. I took a big breath and steeled myself. The train would arrive in one hour.

It is only a fifteen minute walk to the blue bench in the little plastic train-waiting shed beside the tracks, but I like to get places plenty early.

I don't usually go walking around after dark. South Shore is a nice, quiet town, but like most places these days, not nearly as safe as it used to be. I didn't have to worry none after all, though. Bobby Joe had been watching for me and the minute I left my house, he came out of his and said, "How about I carry that suitcase for you, Miss Doreen?"

Someday Bobby Joe is gonna have a big old pot belly like his daddy, but right now, he still has all the muscle he had when he was playing football for the Greenup County Musketeers. Plus he can be as mean as a timber rattler when someone riles him or threatens someone he cares about. Bobby Joe ain't as work-brickle as I'd like, but I surely did feel a lot safer with him walking by my side.

"That would be right nice, Bobby Joe."

He didn't just walk me to the train, he actually waited there beside me all protective-like until the engine came chuffing into town. Bobby Joe has his moments.

I jumped up and tried to wave it down, but the train just kept going. I thought the engineer had gone and forgot me, but the train started slowing down, then the brakes squealed, it came to a stop, and a porter popped out of a silver door. He sat a little yellow step-stool down on the ground and motioned for me to come on.

The train stood still, but it kept huffing and huffing, like it was getting impatient, and I nearly tripped trying to hurry. Bobby Joe grabbed me by my arm and kept me upright. He also handed my suitcase to the porter. The boy hadn't used the wheels even once all this time. He just carried it by the handle like it weighed nothing at all. We grow some strong boys in northern Kentucky.

"You take good care of Miss Doreen here," Bobby Joe told the porter real stern-like. "She's a special lady."

Then them two young men, one white, one black, helped me up them step stairs. I have to admit, my legs were wobbly, and I needed the help. I had barely gotten to the top when the door whooshed closed and the train took off again. I grabbed hold of a handrail sticking out of the wall, and held on while I took a good look down that darkened, narrow aisle with seats on both sides. There was nothing I wanted to do right at that moment except turn around and get right back down off that train! I didn't know where to sit. I didn't know what to do. It seemed like all I could manage was hang on to that hand-hold like my life depended on it while the train swayed and shook beneath me.

Just then, the nice porter started talking to me in a calm, voice.

"Seat number 37, ma'am," he said. "I think that would be a good place for you."

I looked back over my shoulder wondering where Holly's suitcase got to.

"Don't worry, ma'am." He said. "I've got your luggage. Just take it nice and slow and you'll be fine. Your seat is about half-way down the car."

The seats were filled with all kinds of people, most of 'em asleep in miserable-looking positions. Some were light-skinned, some were dark-skinned, some even had them things

I've heard called dreadlocks sticking out of their heads. The lights were dimmed so that everyone could sleep since it was nearly midnight.

It took me awhile, with the train rolling and pitching, before I got my sea legs and could walk half-way steady, but me and the porter finally made it to seat 37 and he lifted my suitcase into the overhead bin. There were even two little bitty white pillows sitting on the two empty seats he took me to.

"The rest rooms are back that way," the porter said. "If you go past the restrooms and into the next car, there's a snack bar. If you need anything, just ask."

I had no intention of bothering the nice young man unless I had to, but I thanked him and settled into the seat. The train was really chugging along now. Getting up speed. It didn't seem real to me that I was actually doing this, so I tried telling myself where I was going so I maybe I could believe it.

"Doreen," I whispered. "Stop being scared. You are truly on a train going to San Antonio, Texas. People do things like this every day and they don't think nothing about it."

It was the first time I'd been more than fifty miles away from home since my class trip to New York City.

Eventually, the soft rocking of the train soothed my nerves, and I started calming down. Then I started getting sleepy. It was after midnight, after all, and my bedtime is nine o'clock, and I was just worn out from all the excitement. I looked over at that extra seat beside me and wondered if there was any kind of rule against laying down sideways and taking me a little nap. I peeked up over the back of my chair. The two seats behind me were empty, and a couple others were empty further back as well, but for the most part people were sprawled out all over the place. So I took them two little bitty pillows, fluffed them up the best I could, kind of laid over on my side, and the next thing I knew I was gone.

I woke up an hour later when the train came to a stop in Cincinnati. I sat up, rubbed my eyes, and watched a whole pack of people rush in. Every seat that weren't already taken had someone storing their suitcases above it. A girl shoved a beat-up duffle bag into the bin above my head, then sat down beside me and introduced herself as Angel. My naptime was over.

The name Angel would normally conjure up the image of a shy, quiet, angelic-looking young girl with blonde hair. This girl named Angel might have been shy and quiet for all I know, but she weren't blonde and she had felt the need to decorate herself with quite a few tattoos like every other young person in the world seems to be doing these days.

I felt like leaning over and saying, "Honey, them ain't going to look so good on you when you're all wrinkled up like Yours Truly."

I didn't say nothing, though. I figured it would be a good idea to keep quiet. It usually is. Someone that young, they think they won't never get wrinkled up. I know this for a fact, because I thought the same way when I was young. Didn't think I'd ever need eye-glasses, either. Or a magnifying glass to thread a needle. When you're young, you tend to think that the only reason people get old is a lack of will power.

Still, the tattoos looked kind of pretty on her skin. If I was younger and my skin didn't sag, I could probably go for a pretty rose or two. The thought made me smile. My mother would have skinned me alive and nailed my hide to the barn door if I'd ever even mentioned doing such a thing.

"Do you want your feet up?" Angel asked.

I didn't have no idea what she meant, so she showed me how I could hit a little lever and a footstool flung up. Then she showed me how to touch another button, and how my seat could go back. It was almost as comfy as my old recliner back home.

I thanked her and we talked for a few minutes. Both of us with our feet up, and our chairs back. She was a nice girl and I was starting to feel real good about taking this trip.

Angel was going to meet her husband, she said. He had a temporary job in Chicago, and she was going up to spend some time with him. She told me that she had a plan. She was going to take a couple pills and sleep until she got there so the time would go faster.

At my age, time going fast ain't always a good thing and I'd already had me a little nap, so I told her I was going to stay awake. That pretty much exhausted our conversation. After taking them two pills, Angel curled up in a little ball on the seat beside me and fell asleep a few minutes after the train chugged out of the station.

It weren't long before I noticed that the little puffy coat she tried to cover herself up with didn't cover up much, poor thing. I was plenty warm so I took my old gray sweater off and covered her with it. She didn't seem to be the kind of girl to take offense at such a small kindness. Besides, it was a little hard to concentrate on enjoying my trip with a dragon peeking out at me from her backside where her shirt had rid up.

I noticed that another girl had gotten on the train with a brand-new baby daughter. So help me, that baby didn't look to be more than a couple weeks old. The girl tried to get a little sleep, but that baby kept needing a bottle or to be jostled around. It cried off and on, and every time it would make a little squawk, the guy with the dreadlocks who happened to be sleeping in the seat in front of me would rouse up, cuss the blue streak and then settle back and nod off again. The young girl would look over at him, like her feelings was hurt, and then go back to caring for her baby.

I felt like thumping that young man on his thick-head for being so rotten-tempered when it was obvious that the poor mother was doing everything she could, but I was fairly certain that thumping a young man in dreadlocks was not a good idea when someone is seventy-one-years-old and wearing a housedress and orthopedic tennis shoes. If Bobby Joe had been sitting beside me, I might've tried it, though. Shoot, Bobby Joe might have thumped him, himself.

To my surprise, that weren't the only baby on our car. Three babies in little plastic carriers was lined up a couple seats up from me. They looked to be triplets about five months old. Pretty children. Rosy cheeked. That mother was all alone, too, but them were the best children. The rocking of the train kept them asleep—or maybe she'd doped them up on Benadryl. I've heard of parents doing that.

Of course, I couldn't help but wonder where the daddies were to all these babies, but that's not something people's supposed to talk about anymore. Where the daddies are, that is.

The swaying of the car made my sweater start to slide off Angel, so I covered her up again and was considering getting a little more shut-eye, when two men I hadn't paid much attention to when they took the two seats in back of me at Cincinnati started talking to each other. I tried not to listen in too closely—that would be eavesdropping—but it's hard not to hear words when someone is talking right behind you. That's one thing that has not started going wrong with my body yet—my hearing.

"Do you think they followed us, Dad?" the younger man asked.

"No." The father tried to whisper, but his voice was gravely and it carried. He sounded like someone who had smoked two packs of cigarettes every day of his life. "If they followed us, we'd be dead by now. That's how those people operate. You don't know its coming until it's too late."

"I wish you never got us into this." The young man's voice was strained. "I'm worried about Nancy and the kids."

"They'll be fine." The father's voice didn't sound sure at all. "Stop worrying."

"I hope you're right." The kid sounded doubtful.

"Wish I could have a smoke," the father said. "It's crazy not letting us smoke on the train."

"I got one of the kids' peppermint sticks in the food bag Nancy packed for me. Would that help?"

"Maybe."

I heard the son rustling around in the bin above us, then the sound of cellophane being peeled off. "Here."

"Thanks," the father said. "Now try to get some sleep. We'll be in Chicago soon."

I have to admit. That whole exchange jarred me. I strained to hear more, but that's all they said.

I glanced at my Timex watch with the big, illuminated dial. It was three o'clock in the morning and we'd been gone out of Cincinnati for quite a while. The son must have been keeping still all this time until he thought everyone in the train would be asleep and he could talk.

My mind started working overtime trying to figure out what in the world them two had gotten themselves into. Then my bladder started to complain. I tried to ignore it, but there are some things that you just can't ignore. It was time to start the trek back to the restroom the porter had told me about, even if I did have to crawl over Angel to get there.

I stood up and tried to get out of my seat so I could get to the toilet, but it took me a long time to maneuver over Angel who was dead to the world. Of course this also gave me time to take a good, long look at the two men behind me. They were most definitely father and son. The father was starting to go bald, although that didn't keep him from having his back hair done up in a ponytail. He wore a sort of green uniform, like the kind you see on a game warden or a forest ranger, except it weren't the whole uniform. It only looked like it might have been part of one, like he might have bought it at a thrift store or garage sale or something. The son was wearing a camouflage jacket and a red baseball cap. They both had what the commercials used to call "five o'clock shadows." The two of them looked to be very rough around the edges, except for one thing. Both had these cute little turned-up noses—the kind a person expects on a cheerleader instead of a grown man.

The dad was laid back in his seat, with a piece of peppermint stick sticking out of his mouth that he was a'sucking on and his eyes were closed. While I was trying to maneuver around Angel, he pulled the stick out for a second, licked his lips, and then stuck it back in. I noticed that the end of the peppermint stick was sucked down to a sharp point instead of being bit off. Guess he was trying to make it last as long as possible. Angel had already confided to me her need for a cigarette and the fact that she wouldn't get to smoke one until we got to Chicago. That was another reason she was trying to sleep the trip away, she said, so she wouldn't sit there craving a cigarette so much.

The son--he looked to be about twenty or so—was laid back in his seat with ear plugs stuck in his ears and wires attached to a little box laying on his chest. Esther has one of them things. I think she calls it an I-pod or an I-pad or something.

So anyways, I made it out of my seat and found the teeny-tiny restroom. It was no bigger than a broom closet. It took a while to figure out how to lock the door and work everything. I managed to take care of business, although in the name of hygiene I did not sit all the way down. I usually don't with public restrooms—too many germs. This toilet was tough to use, though. That seat moved with every turn the tracks made. It was a challenge trying to take aim while the toilet seat moved from side-to-side beneath me, but I did the best I could.

After washing my hands in a sink that was hardly any bigger than a soap dish, I decided to try my luck at the snack bar. It was through two doors that whooshed when I pressed on them. I realized that I'd just passed through one train coach to another and it kinda took my breath away.

The snack person was sitting on a little stool. "What can I get for you?" he said.

I'd given it some thought. I asked for a bottle of water and a candy bar. It came to four dollars, which I found excessive, so I did not contribute any money to the tip jar he had sitting on the counter. I figure he probably made a whole lot more than my social security check anyway. It wouldn't take too much to make more than me.

I kind of spraddle-legged my way all the way back to my seat, holding my balance against the sway of the train. Then I had to straddle Angel to climb over her again. Then I covered up that dragon on her back side again, settled down and took a bite of chocolate and a sip of cold water. I couldn't have been prouder of myself if I'd scaled Mt. Everest.

Then it hit me. What I'd seen out of the corner of my eye while I was getting back into my seat. The boy was gone, and the father was laying kinda different and was awful still.

With a scared feeling in the pit of my stomach, I turned around and peeked up over the top of my seat. Sure enough the seat near the window—the one where the son had sat—was empty, and the one with the daddy in it was—well, let's just say that the peppermint stick weren't sticking out of his mouth anymore.

It was a'sticking out of the side of his neck.

I'm not usually a screaming woman and I saw no reason to

start screaming now. Instead, I swallowed down the bile that was trying to claw its way up out of my stomach, scrambled over Angel as quick as I could, side-stepped past the body and went on a search for the nice porter who had said to ask if there was anything he could do for me.

I most definitely had something he could do for me, and this time I didn't mind asking.

It's interesting watching people try to pretend nothing has happened when something big has happened. The porter didn't hardly know what to do about a man a'layin' there dead with peppermint a'sticking out of his neck and blood all over everything like some stuck pig. The lights were still low, and people were still sleeping all over the place.

"There was a young man with him a'calling him 'Dad,'" I said. "Where'd he go?"

I was back in my seat where I'd had to crawl over Angel again to get to. The girl was so sound asleep I would have been worried about her being dead, too, if she hadn't been snoring. I couldn't help wondering what was in them pills to make her sleep so good.

"We'll take care of this, ma'am." The porter was polite as always, but he dismissed me like I didn't have sense enough for him to even bother talking to. "Please just take your seat."

Mama once said that there was nothing as invisible as an old woman and I've found her to be right. I knew I looked every year of my age and then some. My hair is gray and Holly had given me a fuzzier perm than usual. I've never worried much about skin care. I just wash with soap and water and head back out into the sun to work in my garden. I'm spotted and speckled and wrinkled and exactly the kind of person a young porter would want to ignore. Problem was, I had no intention of that happening.

"Where's the boy?" I asked again, louder. I know I talk with a Kentucky accent, which some people think sounds ignorant, but there's nothing wrong with my mind. I know I didn't dream up no second person in the seat beside of the dead man.

"Please, ma'am," the porter said, and I could tell he was getting a little put out with me.

There was nothing I could do, so I sat down and hoped that the boy with the red ball cap would come back from using the bathroom or taking a stroll or something, but that didn't happen. What did happen was that the train made what the conductor called over the loudspeaker an "unscheduled stop." He told everyone to stay in their seats, and then some police people from whatever town we'd stopped in came aboard to see about the dead man and the porter had to turn on the bright overhead lights, and that waked one of the triplets, and it started crying and that waked up the other babies and they started crying, and the louder they cried, the more they scared the others and before long we had four babies screaming their heads off in our train car, and the man in the dreadlocks roused up and said, "What the..." (I can't print the things he said but I learned a couple new words and I think some other people did, too.)

In the middle of this Angel kinda woke up from her coma and asked, "What's going on?" And I pulled my sweater back up over her and give her shoulder a pat and say "The police are here to take away a man with a peppermint stick a'sticking out his neck."

Angel blinked a couple times, tried to fluff up the little pillow she was using—although them things don't fluff much. Then she said, her voice all drowsy, "that's nice," and fell back to sleep. I made a mental note to find out what it was in them little pills she took. If they're something that can be got in a drug store I'd like to get me some sometime. I don't always sleep as good as I'd like.

Everyone except Angel was full awake, the whole car was watching wide-eyed as the police inspected the body—except I had a ring-side seat because I was turned completely around now, sitting on my knees, watching them do their thing with their rubber gloves on.

"Where's his son?" I try again to make them notice that there oughta be another man sitting there.

No one took no mind of me except an older man in an old brown coat who came on board with them. He weren't dressed like a policeman at all and looked like he got out of bed in a hurry. He took note of me and said, "What do you mean?"

I pointed at the dead man.

"He had a young man sitting beside him who called him Dad. He was laying there asleep when I got up to go to the toilet, and he was gone when I got back and he never showed up again."

The man in the brown coat sidled past the others and planted himself in front of me. Well, Angel, too, but she weren't really a part of the conversation.

"Did you see or hear anything else?" he asked.

Finally. Someone was acting like I maybe got the sense of a goose after all.

"I heard the kid say, 'Do you think they followed us, Dad?' And the father said, "No. If they did, we'd already be dead."

The brown coat man's eyes lit up. "Anything else?"

I repeated the entire conversation pretty much word for word. I have to admit that it was pretty much burnt into my mind.

"Anybody else see anything?" the man in the brown coat asked.

Nobody stepped up to say they had seen anything. It was just as I thought. Everyone had been pretty much asleep.

I was still worried about the boy in the red cap. He weren't a real big kid. Kinda scrawny-looking and short and he'd sounded really worried when he'd talked to his dad.

I added that to my conversation with the man in the brown coat. "I'm really worried about that boy," I said. "He weren't very big. I'm afraid something has happened to him."

The man in the brown coat was nice enough to look me straight in the eyes and agree with me. "I'm worried about him, too, ma'am. That's why I have people already combing all over this train to see if we can find him."

Well, that made me feel a little better. Finally someone was paying attention to the boy. The way I figured it, either he killed his own daddy—which meant he needed to be behind bars, or he had gotten cross-ways of them people he was scared of, or he was off somewhere else on the train not knowing his daddy was dead. Anyway you sliced it, he needed to be found.

As I stood there watching the police people do their thing, I noticed a large man sitting behind the murdered man's seat. He was big in the way that them muscle-men get, not fat, and he was reading one of them hunting magazines that men like. He weren't paying as much attention to what was going on in front of him as I thought most people would be. His nonchalance seemed odd to me.

In the seat next to him, was a person who was obviously still sound asleep, all curled up in a blanket, like Angel was in my sweater. The only thing visible of the big man's seatmate was his nose—a cute little turned-up thing. The kind that you'd expect to see on a cheerleader.

I felt one of them dizzy spells coming over me and I tried to fight it off. Especially when I saw that the big man was holding that magazine upside down. Then he glanced up, saw me looking at him with my mouth hanging open, and I knew that he knew that I knew.

My chest got to pounding and the dizzy spell got worse

and I fell back into my seat and started fanning myself. If I'd thought I was feeling sickish over traveling on this train before I got on, it weren't nothing compared to what I was feeling now.

The man in the brown coat noticed me trying to keep from passing out. He bent way over Angel, his face close to mine.

"Are you okay, ma'am?" he asked.

I emphatically shook my head "no."

"Do you need a doctor?"

I shook my head "no" again and then jerked my head toward the back of the train and motioned with my thumb, trying to tell him that there was something BACK THERE that he needed to investigate AT ONCE!

He glanced at me, then at the big man.

The big man must have figured out something was up, because I heard this commotion back behind me, and some women started screaming, which set the babies off again just when the poor little things had started to quiet down.

"Stop him!" The man in the brown coat yelled.

I forgot all about being dizzy and stuck my head up over the seat again and I saw the man in the brown coat practically climbing over the police people's backs to get past them—everything on the train was so narrow and crammed up. And the big muscled man was lumbering through the train like he was a locomotive, knocking people this way and that. By the grace of God, the little babies were in the front of the car and weren't in the way of any danger. The man in the dreadlocks gave up trying to sleep and just sat there looking at the ceiling shaking his head like he was having a conversation with himself over how bad he was being mistreated on this train trip.

The last I saw of the man in the brown coat, he was headed out the back of the coach with his coat tails flying going after that bad man. Several regular-dressed police people were right behind him.

As soon as the train people could, they uncoupled that train car and set it off to the side so the police could remove the bodies and I surely hope they cleaned them two seats good. They scattered the rest of us throughout the rest of the train wherever there was a seat and we made it back to Chicago a few hours later almost like nothing had happened. I never did see Angel again. We got put in separate cars. I hope she finally woke up long enough to say hello to her husband.

It seemed strange walking into that giant terminal in Chicago. Especially after all that had happened. I finally got to use the little wheels on Holly's suitcase.

I didn't know where to go or what to do again. Then a man driving around on a cart asked me if I was lost, and I said I was. After finding out what train I was going to be waiting for, he put me on the cart and drove me to a counter where they asked me my name. When I told them, the girl behind the counter said that she had a message for me. That the chief of police from some town in Indiana had called with some information for her to give me.

She said the doctors had been able to save the younger man who had been unconscious from the bad man nearly strangling him to death. They'd caught the murderer and he'd told them everything, and it had all had to do with drugs. Everything seems to have to do with drugs anymore, of course. The father in the forest warden clothing actually did work in the park service as a sort of custodian. He cleaned toilets and trails and such. He'd gotten mixed up in some stuff he'd had no business getting involved in.

Turns out that the parks we got in northern Kentucky makes a nice place to hide stuff if you know where to hide it, and he knew all the good places. Some of them have a whole lot of caves in them, and not all of them are well-known to the public. The father had dragged his boy into it with him 'cause the boy had a wife and two children and needed money. The two of them knew they were in trouble and were trying to get away. It turns out that the big man thought it would be funny to kill the father like he did, with nothing more than a sharp peppermint stick to the jugular vein. The boy, leaned so far back in that recliner, had been little effort for the muscle-man to strangle and then slide right off into the empty seat beside him and cover up. It was a deliberate killing meant to send a warning to others who might try to cheat the cartel who had been running the drugs.

It certainly sent a warning to me. I'd been thinking about asking Angel where she got them little pills that knocked her out—but I don't think I want to know anymore.

I thanked the girl for all that information and went over and sat down at a seat she showed me to. It turned out the man in the cart had taken me to an old-fashioned lounge they reserved for important people, or them who had first-class accommodations. The girl behind the counter said I reminded her of her grandma, and then she went and got me some coffee and a doughnut. They had coffee and drinks and doughnuts set out in that lounge place for free.

The train people have been real nice to me. Since the man in the brown coat, who turned out to be a chief of police, contacted them about me they decided a woman my age who had been through the trauma of discovering a dead body on their train, needed to go to San Antonio in more comfort, and since they had extra empty rooms anyway, they upgraded my coach ticket to first-class accommodations and that's why I'm sitting here in my own little private room staring at the Texas landscape as it flies by.

These "roomettes," as they call them, include three meals a

day. I get to go to breakfast, lunch, and dinner in a real dining car with elegant settings and good food instead of that little-bitty snack bar. It feels like I've stepped back in time to a more gracious age than the one I've been living in. I've never done or had anything first class before. I'm a little ashamed to admit that I like it a lot.

During the day I got two nice recliners to sit in. I take turns looking toward the front, and then I switch seats and look out the back. It seems a waste to just use one chair. I found a paperback novel someone left behind that had gotten stuffed in the crack of a cushion. It had a picture of a man and woman on the cover hugging each other. I've always liked a good love-story, but there's things in that book that would curl your hair, so I put it in the little trash bin I got in my room. After I finished it. I hope the porter won't think it's mine. I tried to skip over the curl-your-hair parts, but it was a good story and hard to put down. I'm thinking about reading extra chapters in the Bible to make up for it when I get to Ralph and Carla's.

At night, a different porter than the one I had on the other train comes to turn the chairs into a bed. He makes it up with white sheets all fresh and clean. Then he brings me a new, cold bottle of water to get me through the night.

I've never flown in an airplane before, but I've read about how cramped and miserable people are on them flights, and I'm pretty sure I'd rather travel like this—even if it does take a lot longer. It ain't like I got anything else important to do. It might be nice to see the topside of clouds sometime from a plane, but for my money, not much can beat watching out the window of a train. I had no earthly idea how big our country was. I'll never forgive Ralph for permanently moving far, far away, but I think I'm starting to get an inkling why he wanted to see places and do things he couldn't see or do if he lived forever in South Shore, Kentucky.

I sometimes wonder if I hadn't taken so much time going to the toilet and snack bar if I might have somehow prevented what happened to that young man and his father. Maybe I could have started screaming or something. But I weren't there, and I didn't, and there are just some things in life you have to let go of and leave in the Lord's hands.

There's one other thing about being given this little room that I like. In addition to a nice bed, comfortable seats, free meals, and control of my own thermostat—it has a sturdy lock on the door and I'm using it.

The food on this train is some of the fanciest and best I've ever eaten, but I can't hardly wait to make some plain old bean soup and cornbread for Ralph and Carla. I think I've had quite enough adventure to last me these past three days.

They say that travel changes a person. I know for a fact now that is true. There is no doubt in my mind that I will never taste another peppermint stick again as long as I live.

Murder at the Buckstaff Bathhouse

My name is Doreen Sizemore. I'm a born and bred Kentuckian and I'm seventy-one years old. I still got tolerable good health, all my own teeth, and no cataracts yet that I know of. I been taking care of my sister-in-law for the past few months way down here in San Antonio, Texas. That's where she and my baby brother, Ralph, live.

Frankly, right now I'm so mad at my brother for taking my good nature and hard work for granted that I could just spit. In all my years on this earth I have never minded helping a body out, but I do hate feeling like I'm being used by people, and that's exactly what Ralph's been doing from the moment I set foot in his house until Carla's hair started coming back in after her chemo treatments.

I don't mind helping Carla none, poor little thing. She's one of them women who seem to think that if'n she's real quiet and mousey nobody will notice her and won't bother to hurt her or say something mean to her. I suppose that works in the animal kingdom. If you blend in with the foliage, the hawk won't eat you because it can't see you. But from what I can see, that kind of thinking don't work none too good in a marriage.

While I've been down here, I've been trying to talk to her about standing up for herself a little more. I thought it might help her after I was gone, but it's hard for a woman to stand up for herself when she feels so bad from the chemo treatments she can't even keep down more than a spoonful of Doreen's homemade chicken noodle soup at a time.

So there I was, babying Carla along, cooking one thing after another that might tempt her appetite, when my brother comes home from where he works cleaning out the septic systems of San Antonio, Texas.

"Doreen," he said. "Fix me one of them grilled peanut butter, brown sugar, and banana sandwiches Mama used to make us. You know, the kind Elvis Pressley liked. And while you're at it, how about slicing it diagonal? Sandwiches just taste better sliced diagonal. And I want me some sweet iced-tea, too."

I suppose it weren't a terrible thing he was asking of me. A sandwich and some tea. I mean, Ralph does work hard and it ain't like he's got work that he likes or nothing. He just does whatever he can find that'll pay him a half-way decent pay check. That's what happens when a boy runs off and joins the navy before he's even graduated from high school, and then gets himself kicked out for misconduct. It like to broke me and mama's heart, both of them things did.

Anyway—where was I?

Oh yes. It was the tone of his voice that set my teeth on edge. There was no "please" or "thank you," in his asking neither. It sounded to me like Ralph had stopped appreciating the sacrifice I was making for him and Carla by being all the way down there in Texas and he was starting to treat me like I was some kind of cheap, second-hand, major household appliance.

Truth be told, I was starting to feel like a household appliance and a cranky one at that. I'd been working my fingers to the bone trying to keep that big ole house going he and Carla went and bought, and his stinky work clothes washed and ironed, and groceries in the house, and meals fixed, and dishes washed up, and that weird-looking rat-dog of Carla's fed and let in and out of the door a couple hundred times a day and well, my feet hurt, my back hurt, and I'd just about had it.

Take that dog for instance. Me and him had to come to an understanding early on. He kept out of my way, and I fed and watered him in spite of wishing I'd never laid eyes on the ugly thing. I mean, really. Why would anyone go and breed a dog to look like that? And why would someone actually pay money for him like Carla had?

In my neck of the woods, most people don't pay good money for dogs—mostly, dogs just show up on your doorstep looking for a home. I've had a lot of good porch dogs in my life and not a one of them did I pay for. Of course, they weren't some fancy breed that you could ever tell of. And some of them weren't all that smart. And none of them had any of them papers I hear tell about. But they were fine for petting and barking at people and being sappy-glad each time I come home from the grocery store or my hair appointment, but that's about all I ever needed a dog for anyways.

Thinking of dogs makes me start wondering about how my old tom cat is doing back home in South Shore, Kentucky. Esther, who is married to my second cousin, Bobby Joe, and has a new colicky baby and lives next door is feeding that stray cat for me while I'm down here and I haven't heard from her for awhile.

Funny thing, I miss that cat—bad attitude, open claws, and all. That tom has some scars and some age on him, but he's still spitting, fighting, and surviving. Reminds me a little bit of Your's Truly. I got a few scars of my own and if you try to mess with me, the claws will come out. Guess that's the reason me and that tom get along so well. Neither one of us is going down without a fight and we recognize the warrior in each other's eyes.

Right now, my brother Ralph is fixing to see some big-time claws if he don't figure out his way around a can opener right quick. Goodness! What's he think I do all day that I got time to be a short-order cook for him?

In my opinion, I been here about one week too long. Carla's getting stronger, I'm getting nastier-tempered, and that Ralph has done got on my last nerve. He even left cigarette ashes all over the kitchen table last night and didn't clean them up.

Sometimes, when Ralph is down here in Texas and I'm up there in Kentucky, I get all homesick for the sweet little boy he used to be. I remember all them wilted dandelions he'd bring me in his chubby little hands.

After the first week of cleaning up after his mess, I didn't feel homesick for him no more. That sweet little boy is done and gone and a selfish sixty-five year old man has been left in his place.

Anyway, I told him I was going home, and I also told him that considering how much work I'd done for him, he was going to pay for my train ride. There's only so much my nerves can take. I've just about had it with being gone from home so long, even if I was doing the Lord's work. I mean taking care of Carla is the Lord's work, that is. The Lord's work ain't fixing no Elvis Presley sandwiches for my lazy brother.

"Why not stay awhile longer?" he wheedled. "I'll take you with me to a wine tasting. You know we got real good wine makers around San Antonio now. It's a thriving business."

He said this like I was supposed to be impressed and that made me mad. He knows I'm a teetotaler. Always have been and always will be. Just like my mama. Like my daddy, too, after he got locked away in the county jail that one time for disturbing the peace. That's why my sister, Janice, took little Mira to go see him in jail when she was only two-years-old and the prettiest little thing you ever saw.

"Imagine!" Daddy said after Janice had bailed him out. "A man's grandbaby having to see him sitting there in a jail cell!" He never took a drink again after that one incident and a better man never lived.

Nope. I'm not interested in no wine tasting. I got trouble enough keeping myself on the straight and narrow even with all my faculties still intact.

I tell you what I am interested in, though. I wouldn't mind a'tall seeing the Alamo. We got kin that got killed there. Long way back, of course. At least that's what mama always said and she was a Bowie. She said she was only a real distant cousin, but we always did claim Jim Bowie as blood. He was a Kentucky boy. I read up on him in a magazine once when I was young. Did you know he was sick the day he and his friends lost the battle? He was so sick, he was bedridden, but he died fighting in his bed. They say he emptied both his revolvers into them Mexicans when they came after him and then took that knife of his they named after him and fought until they killed him.

According to the magazine article, when they told his mama that her Jim was gone, she said, "I'll wager no wounds were found in his back."

I always loved that. She knew her boy. Knew he'd never turn his back on a fight. Maybe it was knowing there was Bowie blood flowing in my veins that made me a little bit feistier than some old women. I decided back when I was still a young'n after I read that magazine article that when it came my time to die, there weren't gonna be no wounds in my back, either.

When Ralph invited me to stay another day or two after we saw that Carla was doing better, and offered to take me to that wine-tasting, I told him no-thank-you, but that I would like to go see the Alamo while I was still there in Texas.

Ralph said it weren't nothin' much to see. Not worth taking his day off to go look at a pile of old rocks.

So we got into a big fuss and I told him what I thought of him and Carla took back to her bed with a sick headache and I decided I was going home the next day even if I never did get to see no Alamo.

That Ralph is just spoiled rotten. Me and Janice and mama are probably to blame. We babied him something awful when he was little. It was hard not to. He was a doll-baby with them brown curls and big brown eyes. Ralphie was the sweetest little boy. Once.

Where was I again?

Oh yes. He was just fixing to buy me a ticket back home when my niece (Janice's daughter, Mira, who lives in Arkansas) called to check on Carla. Ralph was a-talking to her, and telling her that Carla was better and that I was going home on the Texas Eagle train, when she let out such a squeal that I heard it coming out of the telephone receiver clear over on the other side of the kitchen.

"Oooh!" she squealed. "Tell Aunt Doreen she's got to come stay with me awhile. The train comes right through Little Rock. I bet it won't cost one cent more for her to stop for a visit. Tell her I said, pretty please."

Now, I have to admit. I was torn. On one hand, I couldn't hardly wait to get back to South Shore, Kentucky and see how my beat-up tom cat and my house plants were faring. (I'd asked Esther to water them, but with that squalling baby, who knows if she remembered a thing I told her about them plants or not.)

On the other hand, I was downright flattered by Mira's enthusiasm for my presence.

Ralph held his hand over the phone receiver. "What do you want me to tell her, Doreen?"

"Oh," I said, putting away the mayonnaise jar from where I'd been fixing myself a cheese and tomato sandwich. "Tell her I'll come for a day or two, but that's all. I gotta get myself back to South Shore one of these days or my house'll forget I live there."

He laughed, but I was serious. I've seen houses just kind of give up when their owners go away for a long, long time. Like they start sagging in on their selves all depressed-looking. I know it don't make no sense. Houses ain't got thoughts or brains or feelings. I know it's just a fancy of mine, but still... I miss my little dump. Me and it has been together a long time.

So I pack up my little red suitcase with rollers that my hairdresser back home, Holly, loaned me and Carla said thank-you and hugged my neck and cried, and Ralph put me on that train the next day. Mira promised to be waiting at the train station in Little Rock, Arkansas to pick me up.

I ain't never been to Little Rock, although I surely did hear enough about it back in the sixties when all that mess happened down there. To tell the truth, I weren't all that impressed with the place when we pulled into town. Like most cities, looks like it just grew without any thought to trying to being pretty.

By the time I got there, I was real proud of how good I'd gotten at traveling by train. I knew how to pull that little foot rest out and everything. I have to admit, though, I did keep a sharp eye out for anything illegal going on. Discovering a dead body on a train like I did on the way down to San Antonio, tends to make a person a tad suspicious.

Oh shoot. I've gone and lost what I was trying to say again. What was I talking about?

Oh yes. Mira. That's what I was talking about. I was going to tell you about that Mira. She was always such a pretty little girl when her mama used to bring her home to visit us in the summer. Bright blue eyes, curly brown hair, and just as pert as you please. Never saw a stranger, that one. She and Janice stopped coming after mama died. I ain't seen Mira since she was in her twenties and Janice passed away and ended up being toted home to be buried. It has hurt my heart some, missing my sister and my niece. Kinda surprised me that Mira wants me to come visit her now so bad.

Mira has not exactly lived a moral life. She eloped with a college instructor half-way through her first year in college, three weeks after he divorced his wife. Made a body wonder just what they had been up to before his divorce. Weren't none of my business, of course. She wouldn't have listened to me anyway. I do some figuring and decide Mira must be a little over forty now. Twenty years is a long time not to see someone you used to teach how to make a blow-whistle out of a blade of grass—but that's what happens when family moves far, far away like Janice went and done.

Yeah, I've missed her. Still miss my sister, too, but that can't be helped.

Anyway, I'm a'looking and a'looking and not seeing her. And then this grown woman who is about ten sizes bigger than the girl I remember hits me like a freight train, a'hugging me and a'crying and carrying-on and saying she's so glad to see me.

I assume this must be Mira but it is a shock. We're a big-boned people but Mira looks like she's been feeding way too good for a long time.

Well now, I'm not exactly a hugging person. Never have been. None of our people ever were. Except Mira's been away a long time and I guess this is one of them habits she's picked up here in Little Rock. Poor little thing. So I hug her back the best I can considering I'm still holding onto my suitcase and the pretty new pocket book straight out of Carla's closet that Carla gave me because it has a strap you can sling around your neck and leave both hands free to travel with.

"This will make things easier on the train," Carla said. "I want you to have it."

I miss that sweet girl already and I'm starting to feel bad I didn't stay longer. I hope she can keep herself fed. That Ralph sure won't help.

After hugging the breath out of me, Mira took me outside and stuffed me into the oddest colored vehicle I ever saw. It reminded me of Pepto-Bismol and made me feel queasy when I looked at it. Mira was proud as punch over it.

"I got this for selling Mary Kay Cosmetics," she said. "I've been the top salesperson in Little Rock now for three straight years in a row."

Well, that explained some things. Now I understood all the make-up on Mira's face. She didn't look bad, exactly. She looked good, but it was easy to see she'd spent an awful lot of time making her face look pretty while the rest of her was hanging out over her skin-tight quintuple X jeans. Poor thing.

"That's real nice," I said.

She chatted along, telling me all about living in Little Rock and all the things they got there that we ain't got in South Shore, Kentucky. Just like her mama, Janice, always did, God rest her soul, who acted like she'd invented living in the big city.

I didn't think it was necessary for her to brag so much. I know I don't exactly live in no thriving metropolis. My neck of the woods is struggling something terrible. If it weren't for government checks and free lunches at the schools, we'd probably all be out in the woods hunting ginseng and frying up possums just to keep body and soul together.

I didn't say anything, though. Just kept nodding and

exclaiming over all the wonders of Little Rock she was telling me about. It seemed to me like she was trying a little too hard to convince me how wonderful things were. There was a bright, shiny sound to her voice like it had some fake inside of it.

The minute we walked into her mini-mansion, she broke down crying and I found out why. She'd been just barely holding herself together. Turns out that college instructor who'd swept her off her feet when she was a freshman had decided he needed his space. He told her he needed some time to figure things out and he'd moved his stuff out lock-stock-and barrel to "find himself."

That had been four months ago and what he'd found weren't himself. It was another college co-ed he'd shacked up with.

I could have told her he would do that in the very beginning if she'd of asked me. Men don't leave a decent wife and a nice house unless they got their eye on somebody else. They just don't. That business of trying to find themselves? That's just husband-speak for I got my eye on somebody a whole lot better-looking than you.

I know these things. I watch my soaps and a body can also pick up an awful lot of good advice at the beauty shop, too. Plus we had us a deacon once down at church who told his wife he wanted to find himself.....but that's a whole other story.

She said he'd asked her just that week for a divorce since he wanted to marry his new little lady love. Mira was so broken up about it, she said all she wanted was her mama to tell her it was going to be all right. Unfortunately, I'm the closest thing to a mama right now that Mira's got.

The girl most definitely needed a shoulder to cry on and my shoulders have sopped up a lot of people's tears over the years. Like I said before, I never resented helping a body out—especially kin—I just take exception to being taken for granted.

So there I was with my coat still on and Holly's little red suitcase still packed, sitting on a couch, a'holding Mira, and her just a' sobbing and boo-hooing something awful, the poor little thing.

I patted and said all the things that a woman says to another woman when things like this happen. Like she's gonna find someone else who'll treat her better and she doesn't deserve this, and that fancy college-teacher husband of hers is nothing but a poop-head. I guess the Lord had known all along that Doreen needed to sit a spell in Little Rock, Arkansas to help Mira get over a broken heart.

I missed Kentucky something awful, though. There's so much heart-break in this world it sometimes makes me want to just go crawl into my little house on the river and lock the door behind me.

I finally got Mira dried up, and I made us some nice rice pudding, which was her favorite when she was a little girl, although I'm afraid that Mira doesn't need a whole lot of rice pudding these days. I didn't say anything while she ate most of the pot, though, alternately licking her spoon and boo-hooing.

We finally got ready for bed, and boy, was I ready to lay my head on a pillow! Looked to me like that mini-mansion of Mira's would have plenty of bedrooms to choose from, but Mira had other ideas. She wanted her Aunt Doreen to sleep with her in her big ole King-sized bed even though I warned her that I snored real bad. She said she didn't care, she was just so tired of being scared and alone.

It was a shame, though. There must have been five bedrooms in that house, and every last one of them, except for Mira's, unoccupied. That's something I don't understand. Why would anyone need that big of a house unless they have a passel of kids?

I actually asked Mira that question. She said it was because her husband wanted them to live in the right zip code which didn't make any sense at all to me. The way I figure it, a zip code is just numbers the post office saw fit to complicate things by making us have to stick them on a letter. It don't have nothing to do with why you pick a house out.

While I tried to parse it all out, she said not to worry about it because she was probably going to lose the house anyway.

I asked why.

She said it was because the house was under water.

That confused me. Her shrubs had looked kind of puny to me when we pulled in, and she'd told me they had been having a drought. It took her some explaining before I understood that they had been paying for ten years on this monstrosity of a house and they still owed more on it than they could get if she sold it.

I know I'm just an old, ignorant, Kentucky woman, but buying ten times more house than you need or can afford just to have the right numbers to write on your envelopes to hand to the postman does not make any sense to me. It made me even more homesick. I love my little two-bedroom house with the yellow kitchen and creaky front porch. Even though whenever it rains too long and the muddy water starts creeping up the river bank fixing to flood, me and my neighbors start worrying about whether our houses might end up underwater for real.

I patted Mira's shoulder and told her not to be afraid. That she could always come live with Your's Truly if she ever needed to. I said that my place might not be fancy, but I could put a roof over her head if she ever needed it. Like I said before, I don't mind helping a person out, especially if that person is kin.

I was trying to make her feel better, but all I managed to do was make the poor girl start crying again.

"Oh, Aunt Doreen," she sobbed. "I'm so glad you're here. I'm so lonely."

Then she hugged the breath out of me again. I was glad when she finished crying herself to sleep. I climbed out of bed real easy-like and made myself a nest in the bedroom next door where I could hear her if she called out for me. I ain't kidding when I say I snore. Shoot, sometimes I get to snoring so loud I scare my own fool self!

Anyway, the next morning, Mira looked like a train wreck when she woke up, but after she got done applying all the stuff from the pink Mary Kay bottles she had on her dresser, she looked pretty good.

Then she said something that stopped me in my tracks. She said she wanted to get out of town for the day and go have a spa treatment and she wanted me to go with her and she wanted me to get a spa treatment, too.

I said I did not want to go.

She said she knew just the spa to take me to that would make me feel all better.

I told her I was not the one who had been feeling bad.

She started crying again.

Now, I've noticed that there's times when deep grief looks a whole lot like crazy. Mira was grieving that low-down snake of a husband of hers something awful, and it was making her a little crazy in the head. I absolutely did not need to have done to me whatever it is that they do to people in them spas in order to feel better. I felt just fine. I felt like a seventy-one year old woman who didn't have nothing wrong with her in the first place.

But when someone you love is hurting that bad, you humor them. You just do. Besides, she said we were only driving an hour away to Hot Springs, Arkansas, which I'd read about in a magazine once and was a little curious about. Plus, I figured she couldn't cry and drive at the same time. I also hoped that whatever they did in them Hot Spring spas might perk her spirits up.

So we packed ourselves up into her Pepto-Bismol mini-van and headed out to get ourselves worked on. I just hoped whatever it was she had in mind wouldn't hurt too bad. I read in one of the them fashion magazines at the beauty shop that some of them fancy places do a procedure called a bikini wax. I'm not entirely sure what's all involved, but it sounds right painful. I decided right then and there that if anyone comes at me with anything involving hot wax, I'm going to respectfully decline. There are some things a body just shouldn't have to put up with in the name of beauty. Ain't likely I'm going to be wearing a bikini any time soon, either.

Shoot, I'll tell you a little secret if you promise not to tell nobody. I accidentally bought me some white bikini panties one time. I hadn't had my glasses checked for a while, and I thought I was getting my regular kind that cover a body up like God intended. It was an accident that I bought them things, but I didn't want to waste my money and I'd already opened up the little plastic bag they came in, so I couldn't hardly take them back to the Dollar store.

I tried to wear them that same morning I opened the package and that was the most miserable Sunday I ever had in my life. Worst thing was, I couldn't do nothing about it. And it was potluck Sunday. I just had to endure them little bitty things a riding up where they shouldn't be riding up until the last casserole dish was washed and dried. Then I got myself home and stuffed them things deep into the trash. I didn't want Horace, who picks up our trash, to see them little panties laying there and start telling people that Doreen had lost her mind and was out trying to find herself a man or something.

Sometimes, in spite of not wanting to live nowhere else,

living in a small town ain't quite what it's cracked up to be--especially when you got to worry about what people might say over what you put in the trash.

Well, I've gone and done it again. Lost my train of thought. I know I did not intend to go down that rabbit hole and start talking about my accidental purchase of bikini panties.

Oh yes—the spa. That's what I was talking about. When we got to downtown Hot Springs, Arkansas, I could surely see why it got that name. Ain't no mystery there. Everywhere you look there are fountains with steam rising off them. Mira told me that people come from miles around to fill up their empty milk jugs with that hot mineral water, and people used to come and soak and soak in that mineral water. Doctors would even write prescriptions for it. How long to soak, and then how long to spend walking along the promenade walkway they had built special for health purposes. Soak, walk, soak, walk.

They called it "taking the waters" and only rich people could afford it. Rich people can come up with the darndest ideas. Sounded like a big waste of time to me, but I'm not judging. Maybe rich people got problems I don't know nothing about.

Anyway, Mira said me and her was going to check into the only remaining bathhouse that gave old-fashioned water spa treatments.

I felt relieved. I'm fine with water—being raised beside of the river and all. In fact, I never feel entirely well when I get too far away from it, although I don't think anyone in their right mind would think soaking in the Ohio River would make them healthier. Too many chemical plants up and down it. No, I'm just relieved because if the Buckstaff Bathhouse is that old-fashioned, I figure there's a right good chance no one is going to try to come at me with hot wax.

Now, seventy-one ain't really all that old compared to, say, ninety. There's things I ain't ever had to do without—like cars and electricity. I'd like to say that stepping into the Buckstaff was like stepping back into time, but it weren't any time I'd seen in my day. You could tell that this had been one fancy, expensive place in its day.

First off, everything was marble and tile. Little bitty tile on the floor in fancy shapes and designs. I stood there admiring it in the foyer while Mira made the arrangements at the desk for our spa treatment. Mira said it was a gift from her to me for listening to her caterwaul last night for so long.

There was some Asian people paying for the water treatment, too, a girl and a young man. We had to wait while they got their English sorted out and everyone understood each other. Then we got on an elevator with a cage-like door that they closed and a girl sitting there on a stool operating it. That was a different experience all in its own self. I'm just barely old enough to remember there being an elevator operator at that fancy Marting's Department store over the bridge in Portsmouth, Ohio back when I was a kid.

The girl was real nice as we went up to the second story. It turns out that women had a whole floor to theirselves. The men's was on the main floor, the women's on the second, which didn't seem fair, but I try not to complain unless it's really important.

We got up there on the second floor and there was these big, open, echoey spaces everywhere with lots of light. Nothing smelled like chlorine, neither, like it always did over at Portsmouth at the Dreamland pool I used to go to as a kid. Nope. The whole place just smelled like pure water. And everywhere I looked underfoot there's all these fancy tiles and I think of the hours it must have took to get them fancy tiles placed just right.

Mira really should have prepared me better for what came

next, but she didn't. The elevator girl took each of us to a little tiny dressing room with two skinny lockers in each of them. There was a white wooden chair to sit on, and a key she showed me how to use and then loop over my wrist with a stretchy, plastic thing.

"Take off all your clothes. Put them in here. Lock the locker. Then wait for someone to come put a sheet around you," the elevator girl said and left.

Now, this put me in a quandary. When she said "take off all your clothes" did she mean ALL my clothes?

"Mira," I said through the petition. "Did she mean..."

"Yes, Aunt Doreen. Underwear, too. You're going to be getting into a bathtub."

So I took off even my skivvies, stuffed everything into the little locker, locked it, looped the key around my wrist, memorized the number 40 that was on the locker, and then sat down on that white painted wooden chair. I was just as naked and goose-bumpy as a raw turkey and I was not happy about it. Then I started wondering how many other bare bottoms had sat on that painted wooden chair, and I stood up real quick again.

Goodness! The things I get myself into trying to be nice to people! If I'd known listening to Mira boo-hoo last night would cause me to end up like this, I'd have turned around and gotten back on the train.

Just about the time I got ready to give up and put my clothes back on, some woman came to the curtain and said, "knock knock."

Now, all I'm saying is it's hard to know exactly what to do when all you got on you is goose flesh and some strange woman says "knock knock" into your curtain.

A need to say "who's there" came over me, as well as a desire to giggle at all this silliness Mira was putting me through, but I stifled my need to try to be funny and just said, "Come in."

"Turn your back to me, honey," the woman said, without opening the curtain. "And raise your arms."

So I did that. Feeling like a dad-blamed fool the whole time. I seen some long, black arms whip a sheet around me quick as could be, and then the woman flipped the edges over my shoulders in what she called "a toga."

"Now turn around and follow me," she said, in a real kind voice. "My name is LaToya and I'll be taking care of you today."

LaToya was about my height, had pretty, braided hair, and a real nice smile on her face. She must have seen the look of I'm-not-so-sure-about-this on mine because she tried to reassure me. "It's going to feel real good. I promise."

Next thing I knowed, she's taken me to another little cubicle with a big, white, claw-footed bathtub big enough for three people to sit in. Seems like overkill for just me. It was filled with water and there was a little footstool for me to step up into it. I tried to take my sheet in with me, but she pulled it away and there I was, climbing into a bathtub as stark naked as a two-year-old getting a bath by its mother.

I stepped into the mineral water and almost stepped right back out again. It was almost—but not quite—scalding hot. I kinda danced around some before I decided I could stand it to sit down, but it weren't easy. LaToya had me sink down into it and stretch out until my toes were touching the bottom of the bathtub underneath the faucet, and she laid some kind of a board behind my back to relax onto, and she stuck a rolled up towel behind my neck, and then she turned something on that looked like my cousin Benny's little outboard trolling motor. It started riling up the water something serious.

"You just relax now," LaToya said, and closed the curtain to my little cubicle.

I have a confession to make. I was raised with no bathtub at all. No shower neither. We washed ourselves in the river most weeks. In the winter I was raised taking a once-a-week all over bath in a tin tub in the same water Janice and Ralph had theirs.

When a person grows up without a bathtub, you never really get over the luxury of having one and I finally let myself relax and just luxuriated like I knew Mira and LaToya was wanting me to.

That water felt so good a bubbling away. Kinda made everything I'd been through the past weeks drain on out of my body.

I was just about to doze off when LaToya says, "Knock Knock" again and brought me in two little plastic cups of mineral water. "Just sip it" she said. "It's warm."

Well, I started to sip it and was shocked that it was as hot as the bathwater.

"It comes straight out of the ground like that," she explained. "It's just mineral water and real good for you."

So I sipped down two plastic glasses of water so hot you could of stuck a Lipton tea bag in it and made tea. Then LaToya left me alone again and I sunk down deep into the water and for the next twenty minutes I felt like I was one of them rich women who used to come and spend weeks here.

"Knock Knock," LaToya said, from outside the curtain. "Bathtub time is up."

I hated to leave that big old bathtub, but she was right. It was time. The heat had already made my legs a little wobbly. LaToya helped me out, wrapped me back into my sheet, and we went marching off to what she called a sitz bath. By this time, I had lost all track of Mira and I was beginning to lose track of time, too. I was starting to warm up to just doing whatever I was told because everything I was being told to do was feeling awfully good.

Then LaToya had me put my shiny-hiney right smack down in a porcelain seat full of hot water. She leaned me back, stuck my feet on a towel-covered footstool, and draped me with that sheet again. This, she told me, was supposed to limber up my lower back. She forgot to whip the curtain closed this time and for a few minutes, I had a view and could see what all was going on around me.

There was one young woman lying quietly on a blue, cushioned, table who was kinda interesting. I knew I had seen her before. She was the small, Asian girl who had been signing in ahead of me and Mira when we came through the front door. It surprised me that she had chosen to wear a purple bathing suit underneath her sheet. I had no idea a bathing suit was allowed in this place. This one weren't no two piece either. It was a one-piece with a skirt.

"Oops!" LaToya walked by and whipped the curtain shut. "Sorry about that."

Once again, I was enclosed in my little cubicle, which was fine with me. I hadn't gotten all that much privacy at Ralph and Carla's. I liked the feeling of being in this little cocoon.

I hate to admit it now, but I spent just a little time feeling superior to the Asian girl because I had started feeling like an old hand at that sheet business. I was enjoying the whole process and didn't need the prop of a purple bathing suit to feel comfortable.

LaToya came back in about ten minutes about the time my lower back started feeling all loosey-goosey. Then I got the mummy treatment over where the Asian girl had been a few minutes earlier. Hot, wet towels were wrapped around my feet and legs and behind my back and neck, and then LaToya put a nice cold towel over my forehead, and handed me two glasses of iced mineral water to drink.

After I'd downed all that water, she laid me back and covered me up with that sheet again.

"I'll be back in ten minutes," she said.

Okay, I admit it. I fell asleep and didn't know nothing at all until she woke me up and broke the bad news that the steam cabinets were not working. I took a look at the metal, closet-looking things with a hole for a person's head to poke through and decided that I was fine with the fact that they were broke.

She took me to this needle shower, which shot at me from all directions from the top of my head to my knees for two minutes. It was like being in a waterfall and I could hardly get my breath. Then LaToya dried me off, wrapped that sheet around me one more time—it was starting to get a little wrinkled and draggy by now--and left me sitting in the room where I'd get a massage.

Except for a few hugs at church now and then, I don't get touched a lot, and I weren't sure I was going to be comfortable having some stranger a'rubbing on me, but a nice lady named Tracy started working out all the kinks in my shoulders and back and asked me what in the world I'd been doing to be so knotted up.

That's all she asked, but it surely did unleash a flood of words. I don't know what got into me. I started telling her everything. She heard about my selfish brother, and Carla, and that whole mess of finding a dead body on the train to San Antonio. Don't know if she bothered to listen to a word I said, but by the time that girl was done, I was purring like my old stray tom cat the first time I gave him a whole can of tuna all for his own self.

I'm not sure I'd ever have gotten off that table if she hadn't told me she was done. She showed me the way to the locker rooms, me with that sheet wrapped around me, dragging it behind me like a draggled-tail chicken, but happy as a clam I was feeling so good.

I pulled the curtain closed behind me, dropped my sheet on the white wooden chair, inserted my handy-dandy little key that was dangling from the twisty thing on my wrist into the lock, and the locker didn't open.

I grabbed hold of the locker handle and shook it a bit trying to get it unstuck. That's when I realize two things at once. I had stuck my key into number 39 instead of number 40, and there was a tiny piece of purple shiny material sticking out of number 39. Unfortunately, my shaking had loosened the door enough that it suddenly flung itself open and a body came tumbling out.

Someone had gone and stuck that little purple-bathing-suited Asian girl inside that locker. I know it only took about a second, but for me, time stood still. I watched that poor girl unfold out onto the floor like it was a slow-motion movie.

I hate to admit it, but I acted like a complete nut. I grabbed my damp sheet, held it up to my chest like it could protect me from whoever had done this terrible thing, and then I backed out of that little cubicle screaming my fool head off.

After that, one of my dizzy spells hit. As I passed out flat on the floor my last thought as I lay there was, "Somebody sure did put a lot of time and thought into laying out this pretty tile floor."

It ain't every day that a dead body is found in the Buckstaff. In fact, I think this might have been the only time ever. Lucky me. I sure hope I don't become a murder magnet like that Miss Jane Marple in all them Agatha Christie novels I used to read when I was a girl. I remember thinking that if I was one of Miss Marple's friends I'd a'high-tailed it away from that woman as fast as I could since there always seemed to be a dead body showing up every time she took a trip or went to a party.

I woke up from my dizzy spell shivering something awful, with Mira sitting there on the floor in her street clothes patting me and telling me to wake up and one of them police women feeling for a pulse like she thought I was dead. I sat straight up and saw a policeman kneeling beside the dead body and the staff standing around looking upset and miserable. I was awful relieved to find out that Mira had managed to cover the important parts of me up with that sheet. Pretty sure I didn't accidentally land all that modest.

An Asian man was crying in the corner with a policeman standing there patting him on the shoulder. I recognized him as the man who'd stood in front of us at the desk while the Asian woman signed them in. He was damp and disheveled and looked like he'd just been drug up from the floor beneath where the men-folk got their spa treatments.

I glanced up at LaToya. Her face was set in stone and she didn't look at me or smile. Tracy weren't paying any attention to me either, even though she'd been awful kind-acting when she was giving me my massage. Only Mira seemed to really care that I was laying there on the floor. When you get right down to it, the only people you can depend on is nearly always your own kin folk.

"How are you feeling Aunt Doreen?" Mira asked.

"With my fingers." I weren't really trying to be smart-alecky, I just didn't want to get into a rehash of my dizziness problem right now. "I need my clothes."

"They won't let you have them yet," Mira said. "Your clothes are in the locker where they have everything taped off. And...that girl hasn't been moved yet."

"I need me some clothes." I insisted.

"Can my aunt have her clothes?" Mira asked the nearest

officer. "She's cold and she's had a shock." Her voice took on a warning tone. "Her son, Owen, is an attorney and has a real short fuse when it comes to his mother. I sure wouldn't want to be you or the owners of the Buckstaff if Miss Doreen here ends up in the hospital over this."

"Owen?" I blinked. That fall must have knocked something loose in my brain. I didn't remember having a son, let alone one named Owen.

"Yes, Aunt Doreen." Mira winked at me real solemn and meaningful-like. "You know how Own gets when it comes to you and your health."

It weren't right for her to lie like that, but as fast-thinking as Mira was, I could see why she was such a good saleswoman that she got to drive a pink mini-van around the city. The mention of my new son, Owen-the-lawyer, made the staff make things move fast.

The next thing I knew, I was dressed in the same kind of clothes that the staff wore—kind of like them shirts and pants that nurses wear—except these had the Buckstaff logo on them instead of little tiger and fishies like some of the nurses wear back home over across the bridge at Southern Ohio Medical Center. Someone even found me a pair of clean fuzzy socks and some slippers. Some underwear woulda been real nice, too, but beggers can't be choosers.

Like I said. The staff was all there, crowded around. Their expressions were a combination of being sick at heart, and sheer curiosity.

"Who was in charge of this dead woman?" one of the cops asked.

LaToya stepped forward. "Me."

"Do you have any idea what happened to her?"

"No, sir," LaToya said. "I'd left her sitting in the massage room to wait for Tracy to finish with Miss Sizemore."

Tracy spoke up. "When I finished with the Sizemore woman and came out to get the girl who ended up....well, you know... she wasn't there. Me and LaToya both thought she'd changed her mind about the massage and went home. That's happened a few times when someone getting a massage groans a little too hard."

At that point, Tracy shot a stony glance at me like I'd done something wrong. Well, I might have groaned a little. The massage had felt good. I was just trying to let her know I appreciated it.

A policeman started questioning me then and I wished I had something to tell him, but I didn't. Just that I got mixed up on the lockers and had found a dead girl in one of them. I left out the part about me screaming my fool head off. I did not think it had any bearing on the case.

Mira wanted to get me out of there but I dug in my heels. Maybe it didn't matter to her, but I wanted my own clothes that I'd stuffed in that locker, and I was going to wait until they let me have it. My pocket-book that Carla gave me was in there, too. It didn't have a lot of money in it, but it did have my driver's license and even though I can't drive real good anymore because of the dizzy spells, I didn't want to lose it. I was afraid the people at the DMV wouldn't give me another one.

About that time, I saw a man coming in dressed in street clothes. He took one look at the dead girl sprawled out on the floor in her purple bathing suit and let out a loud sob.

"Darling!" he said. "Who did this to you?"

Of course, she didn't answer because of being dead and all.

Then he started fighting his way toward her while staff and police people tried to hold him back.

I kept wracking my brain, trying to figure out why he looked so familiar. I lost track of Mira for a while. Then I saw she'd wandered off and was looking out the window at the city of Hot Springs. Just as well. Things were getting kinda cramped where I was.

"Mira?" I walked over to her, just as the man collapsed onto the floor, sobbing and LaToya tried to offer him a cup of that iced hot mineral water. "Are you okay?"

"Yes." She turned her face toward me and I saw she'd been crying again. "It's just so crowded I thought I'd get out of the way. Are you ready to leave now?"

"I was ready to leave the minute that girl's body came falling out of the locker."

"Good," she said. "I'll head on downstairs and bring the car up to the front so you won't have to walk so far."

"What about my pocketbook and things?"

"Give them this." She handed me her pink Mary Kay business card. "Tell them to call us when they're finished and I'll come get your things."

They were so busy trying to calm the man down, the police woman who had been patting my hand didn't pay a whole lot of attention when I handed her Mira's pink card.

"We'll be in touch," she said, and slipped it into her pocket.

Mira didn't make me sleep in the king-sized bed with her that night. She'd calmed down some by then. I figured that maybe getting dunked in all that mineral water had been good for her.

As for me, although all that mineral water had felt real good at the time, I was all knotted up again because of finding that poor dead girl's body. I couldn't stop thinking about who could have done it. LaToya was a big woman, but she weren't fat. She was muscular. I'd felt that strength when she helped me get out of that big bathtub.

Tracy was a strong woman, too. You'd have to be strong doing all the massaging she done in a day. It took some muscle to put the kind of pressure on my back that she'd done. And to do that all day long every day? She had to have some strength.

I had heard one of the policemen saying they thought the girl's neck had been broken. It takes some strength to break a person's neck. How do I know this? Because I used to help Mama wring chicken's necks before cooking them for Sunday dinner. A human neck had to be a lot harder than that because a chicken's neck is a lot skinnier.

LaToya hadn't been looking all that sympathetic when I'd seen her standing there. Tracy had just seemed annoyed. I hadn't seen enough of the other staff members to read them very well.

I wished I could figure out who had killed the girl, and then go talk to the police about it, but I weren't a Miss Marple who could astonish the police people with her clues and revelations. I was just plain Doreen Sizemore from South Shore, Kentucky who had the bad luck—twice—of finding a dead body where there shouldn't be one.

Even though I was as tired as a tail-chasing hound dog, I didn't sleep well that night. It weren't only because of the murder either, even though that didn't help my peace of mind none. I hate to admit it in mixed company, but I got the trots that night. Bad.

If you don't know what "the trots" are, that's Kentucky-speak for having to go number two a lot. It comes from trotting back and forth to the outhouse. Except I didn't have to use the outhouse. I had my pick of Mira's four shiny bathrooms. I was too sick to appreciate having so much variety. I just used the one right beside my bedroom. An old woman doesn't always have the best control in the world and I figured I'd better get there fast. My stomach cramped and hurt all night long.

Well, I didn't die that night. In the morning Mira got on her computer, did a little reading, and told me that from what she could see, sometimes people get diarrhea when they have a good massage because it releases poisons in their body and them poisons have to come out somewhere. That was news to me. If that was what was happening, I surely must have had a lot of toxins in me and I knew who to blame—namely, Ralph. That brother of mine would make anyone's body toxic.

Mira left early that morning on an emergency beauty call and left me to finish my toast and jam all by my lonesome.

I was finishing the dishes and pondering what a beauty emergency was, when the doorbell rang. I didn't know how to load Mira's dishwasher, so I was washing them by hand. I dried my hands off with a dishtowel and went to answer the doorbell, but I was careful. I made sure I looked out the window first. I saw two police people, a woman and a man standing there.

Now I seen enough TV shows to ask to see their badges— which they showed me. Problem was, I never seen a badge close up before so I didn't know if they was real or not. For all I knew, them badges could have been out of a Cracker-Jack box. But they looked real, and the police people looked real, so I took a chance and invited them in.

I hoped maybe they'd brought my things from the locker, but they said my things would have to stay at the crime scene a while longer. I couldn't see how my skivvies and dog-eared social security card could help them with figuring out who killed Miss Purple Bathing Suit, so I wished them good-luck with that.

They didn't seem to be in any hurry to leave, though. So I tried to be patient and wait for them to come out with whatever it was they wanted to say. They asked where Mira was and kinda smiled when I told her she had gone to help someone who was having a beauty emergency, her being a Mary Kay consultant and all.

What they said next threw me for a loop, though. They wanted to search the house.

I was just flabbergasted. Search Mira's house? What did they think they were going to find? An illegal shade of lipstick?

I gave them permission though. I knew Mira didn't have nothing to hide except a broken heart, and my own life has always been an open book. It's had to be, living in South Shore and all where everyone knows everyone else's business pretty much all the time. At least it's been an open book up until them accidental bikini panties I stuffed down deep in the trashcan so Horace wouldn't see them.

Anyway, they made a sort of hunt through the house, but the only thing they took was Mira's computer that was in her bedroom. I tried to protest, saying she used it for her Mary Kay business, but they said they needed it. I told them I was pretty sure Mira would be mad about that. They said to call my son, Owen, the attorney if she had a problem with it. It might have been my imagination, but it seemed like one of the officers kinda smirked when he said that--like he knew Owen was a figment of Mira's imagination.

I felt bad about that. I was kind of warming up to the idea of having a son named Owen.

Well, seeing that computer walk out the door in the arms of the police was pretty upsetting to me because I knew it was all my fault. I should have told them they needed a search warrant instead of just letting them look around inside like the dummy I am. Even though I don't have no attorney son I ain't completely ignorant about the law. I watch TV.

I wandered into Mira's bedroom after that and stood there and stared at the spot on the table where she'd kept her computer. I kept wishing I could go back and do things differently from the moment the doorbell rang. For one thing, I probably would have minded my own business and not opened the door.

Mira had made a little office out of one corner, even though she had rooms to spare, and it surely looked bare without the computer there. Then I noticed something else about her room. There was a picture missing. I remembered it from the first night I'd stayed with her in her room while she boo-hooed.

Suddenly, it struck me. That is why the man in the bathhouse had looked so familiar. He'd been the man in the picture but aged several years. I hadn't recognized him right off because he'd been dressed in a white tuxedo in the picture.

Now, I know it seems strange that I wouldn't recognize my own nephew-in-law except a lot of years had gone by since it was taken. Plus a tuxedo can make an even big difference in a man's looks. I hadn't attended the wedding because it was so far away and as far as I could remember, my sister had never sent me a picture of Mira's husband. The framed photo that had been on Mira's dressing table was the only time I had laid eyes on the man.

For a minute or two, I pondered why she hadn't acknowledged him while he was down on his knees, and sobbing in the bathhouse. And then I pondered what the connection was between him and girl in the purple bathing suit. And then I pondered over how Mira had turned away while he was there. And then I pondered about the fact that Mira had kind of disappeared early-on in the whole bath house experience.

As everything came together in my mind, I got a bad chill down the back of my neck. I didn't wait. I took off out of that house like a bat out of hell and thanked the Lord Jesus that the policemen hadn't quite finished settling the computer into the trunk of the patrol car yet when I came barreling out of that house and didn't stop until I was right beside that squad car.

"You got room for one more?" I said, panting. "I don't want to wait around for Mira to come home. Not anymore."

After a few questions, they stuffed me in the back of that police car and took me to headquarters where I felt a whole lot safer than I did sitting there in Mira's house waiting for her to come back.

Like I said before. The line between deep grief and crazy sometimes gets a little blurry.

Turns out that Mira had managed to hack into her husband's e-mail account (he'd used the name of his new girlfriend as his password, the big dope) and she'd read the e-mail between them where they were chatting about the girlfriend taking her brother, who was visiting from Japan, to the Hot Springs Bathhouse the next day at ten o'clock. Turns out them Japanese people like their hot water soaks. Mira's husband said he didn't want to do the bathhouse, but he would meet her and her brother afterward for lunch at a certain restaurant near there.

Mira hadn't been trying to be good to me after all. She'd planned to go to that bathhouse all along so she could get a good look at that girlfriend of her husband's. She'd planned to confront her and ask for her husband back, but Mira told the police later that the minute she got a good look at that skinny little body, she'd just snapped in the head and twisted that skinny little neck real hard without thinking.

Too late, I remembered Janice telling me about Mira taking some kind of karate when she was a teenager and how she'd been real good at it, too, but I had forgotten all about that. She hadn't looked much like a karate person when she picked me up at the train station.

Mira said when she'd seen what she'd done, she wanted to cover it up fast before someone found the girl. She looked around and there was no one to see her, so she'd stuffed the girl—who probably didn't weigh more than eighty pounds--in the first empty locker she came to. Too bad it had to be next to mine. She thought it would give her more time to get out of there than risking someone else coming in and finding her. Mira didn't sound like an adult woman when she was talking about any of this. She sounded more like a little kid who had broken a dish and hid the pieces hoping no one would find out.

It was a mess.

After I got in the police car, they put out an APB (that stands for All Points Bulletin in case anybody don't watch the television set like I do) for Mira's car. They found her two states over trying to make her get away. Poor thing. It's kinda hard trying to blend in with the traffic when you're driving a Peptol-Bismol-pink mini-van. The Mary Kay training doesn't include how to hot-wire and steal someone else's car when the pink one is making you stick out like a sore thumb.

Turns out there had never been a beauty emergency. Mira had taken off and left me stranded there at her house with no way to get to the train station at all. If the police hadn't come, I'm not sure how long I'd have sat there waiting for her to come home.

Mira is in a facility for the mentally deranged now. She wrote me the other day and reminded me of my promise to let her move in with me if she ever needed a place to live. She wanted to know if the offer still held good.

I ain't no coward, and if push comes to shove, just like Jim Bowie, there won't be no wounds in my back, but I'm thinking that if Mira gets out any time soon, I might have to go visit Ralph and Carla again.

Ralph ain't such a bad guy. Not really. Fixing him a Elvis Presley sandwich now and again don't seem like all that bad a thing right now.

Not if Mira ever heads my way again.

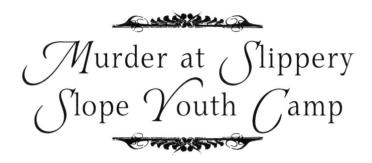

Murder at Slippery Slope Youth Camp

Some people love to travel. But me? I flat out hate it. The way I look at it, my home town of South Shore, Kentucky is one of the few places left on earth that still makes sense and I ain't in no hurry to leave it. With all the talk about gun control, I'm thinking that they'll have a hard time prying guns out of all the good old boys' hands we got around here. It's one of the many reasons I only feel safe when my feet are planted smack dab on Kentucky soil.

It used to be just the Communists we were supposed to fight if they come over here. That was back when life was simple. Now it seems like there's threats all over the place. These days I've started losing track of who I'm supposed to be scared of. There's ISIS, of course. And North Korea keeps making noise. China is a big worry, too. Then there's the finger-pointing back and forth between the Democratic Party and the Republican Party and now we got us the Green Party, the Libertarian Party, and the Tea Party. Heard the other day there's somebody trying to get something started called the Coffee Party.

Sometimes it seems like everybody in Washington is having

themselves a party except us regular folks just trying to make ends meet.

I can only get two channels on my TV set and they're a little fuzzy. People at church tell me I should sign up for cable but them two channels I get right now are enough to worry a person to death—especially if you watch the news much. Them news people don't seem to have a whole lot of good news to tell us about.

That's why I like living in Kentucky. We still got a few people who know how to go out in the backyard on Sunday morning, kill a chicken and turn it into dinner before putting their church clothes on. I'm one of them people. I know how to turn a young ground hog into fritters, too, or make venison taste like prime beef. Kentuckians like me know how to survive whether we got a grocery store or not...although I do like me a Moon Pie every now and again. Moon Pies don't exactly grow on bushes.

Now, what was I talking about?

Oh yes, them people in Washington D.C. What a hot mess that place is! I seen a lot of elections come and go over the years and I surely hope the good Lord has things under control because it's clear to me that there's a lot of folks in Washington who hardly know how to dress their own selves, let alone run the country.

I've seen a lot of elections come and go because I ain't no spring chicken. I'm seventy-one year's old and I say the word "old" because people who say things like they're seventy-one years "young" or try to pretend they're having their 39th birthday for the umpteenth time just flat out annoy the tar out of me. As hard as I've worked I figure I've earned credit for every last one of them years.

I got me a little house that ain't much to look at. The roof sways a mite, and there's a couple of boards on my front porch that it would be wise not to stand on if you ever come visit. My old house is all paid for though, and the tax people decided a long time ago that it weren't worth much so the taxes are real low. I thought about getting it painted last year but I was half-afraid if I did fancy it up a mite the tax people would come sniffing around again and as you probably know that is never a good thing. As it is, I get enough money from my social security check to just about live on if I'm real careful. Fortunately, I got tolerable good health and can still do for myself so I don't need a lot.

I say "tolerable good" health because if I told the truth to people and said that I'm as healthy as a horse I'm pretty sure people around here would plumb work me to death. In case you're worrying, I've been to see the doctor about that little dizzy spell I had awhile back and all he says is that's to be expected at my age and to go ahead and do what I want to do. He said I got me a slight blood sugar problem and all I needed was to eat healthy snacks more often, so that's all right. I did not mention my affection for Moon Pies. I didn't want to worry him. I like my little doctor. He's learning to speak English real good.

Now where was I again? Oh yes. How people would work me to death if I ever told them I was as healthy as a horse.

I know what you're thinking. You're thinking who's gonna work Doreen to death when she don't have no family to speak of living close by anymore? No kids. No grandkids. No husband to pick up after. All she's got is her own self and how hard can that be?

Anybody who thinks that ain't never been part of a country church. Little country churches are all over the place here in northern Kentucky. Most of 'em are just a' hanging on. Too many young people moving away to other places to get better jobs. Them that don't move away, well, I hate to say it, but an awful lot of 'em ain't all that work-brickle anyhow.

Of course why should they bother to work hard when they can sit around cashing checks from the government while they study up on how to make that crystal meth stuff that's just about ruint our country? I never saw the like of what's happening these days. Why, the other day I saw an advertisement for people on the dole to come get their selves a free phone.

Makes me so mad I just want to spit. Shoot—I don't even have no telephone and I worked most of my life over the bridge in Portsmouth at that Selby Shoe factory until it shut down. Sewed right through my own fingers a couple of times, too, when I weren't paying attention. Then I got a job clerking at the grocery store in town. That was a pretty good job and I liked it. Got to talk to a lot of people and the drawer weren't never short-changed when Doreen was behind it, I'll tell you that! I earned every blessed dime I ever spent.

I'm not a hard-hearted woman but I'm getting awful confused about the world I'm living in these days. In my opinion, I tend to think that giving people a hoe and a packet of seeds might be a lot better investment instead of a free phone.

Anyway, about country churches working a person plumb to death. My friend, Ella, is only two months younger than me and she made the mistake of saying she had too much time on her hands one Sunday morning in the foyer. Before she knew what had happened, she ended up in charge of Vacation Bible School.

Frankly, I'd rather try to pet the old stray tomcat who comes mewling around my door than be put in charge of Vacation Bible School. That tomcat has got a wicked left hook if you try to pet him. I know this because I still got the scars. I feed him anyway, but he's like some people I've met--don't try to get too close or they'll rip your head off.

So it was right after church and me and Ella were getting caught up with each other a'talking in the back of the church building and I was offering to bake any amount of VBS cookies for snack time if only she wouldn't make me teach a bunch of squirming little kids. Then I glanced up and saw our new preacher headed our way, looking like he planned to talk with me.This does not usually happen. Me and him have a near-perfect relationship. He preaches. I tell him his sermon was good. He asks if I am well. I tell him I'm tolerably well. And if all goes according to plan, I never think about him or see him again until the following Sunday.

"Sister Sizemore," he said, real polite. "I've been wondering if you would consider coming along with us on a youth outing I have planned for this spring."

I pushed my glasses back up the bridge of my nose and looked at him to see if he'd lost his senses.

"Me?" I say. "Tagging along with our youth group? Shoot, I didn't even get all that involved with the youth group when I actually was a youth."

It's the truth. Except for that time when I was eighteen and helped ride herd on the younger kids at church camp, I been a home body for as long as I remember. Which is why one of the few times I ever set foot outside of Kentucky was this year when I took that trip to San Antonio, Texas on the train and found a dead body...which just goes to show you that it don't pay to travel.

Anyway, just because I solved that mystery and accidentally got myself writ up in the local newspaper I've been kind of a local celebrity ever since. As you might can tell from that, it don't take a whole lot to impress people in a little place like South Shore, Kentucky. Shoot, Velma Whittaker wrote a book about child-raising. She paid four-thousand dollars to get it printed, and has been selling it out of the trunk of her car ever since trying to recoup her investment. There was a real big write up in the paper about Velma being an author.

I might have been more impressed with her book if I didn't know Velma's kids. Stinkers, every last one of them. I wouldn't give you a dollar for the whole blessed tribe.

Now, where was I?

Oh yes, Reverend Jimmy Bell, our new little preacher from Michigan, was wondering if I would like to come along and help out on a youth outing.

Before I tell you the rest of this story, I think I need to tell you about our church. Back when I was a girl it was called The Little Faith Evangelical United Brethren church and we were pretty sure we were the only ones going to heaven. I remember feeling sorry for them liberal Methodists and their wrong ways. Then somebody somewhere decided we needed to combine forces with the Methodists and suddenly I was attending The Little Faith United Methodist church. Now, this was a shocker, but I dealt with it pretty good for a lot of years. Then things changed again.

The United Methodist Church went and got behind some things that were a whole lot more politically correct than scriptural and my friend Ella and some others got all upset about it and they went to some kind of a meeting and read some Bible scripture against it and the powers-that-be told them to be quiet and sit down and Ella got hot under the collar and said some things she probably shouldn't have and the upshot of it all was that our church resigned from the United Methodist Church.

The bad thing was, we also lost our building that we bought and paid for these past hundred years. They told us we could have it back, but we'd have to pay them for it, so we had some fund raisers and were finally were able to buy it back and now it's all ours and nobody can take it away from us. There's a new sign over the door of our building now that says, "Little Faith Community Church."

I'm not real sure what we believe these days, but I'm pretty certain nobody thinks we're the only ones going to heaven anymore. If they do, they're keeping it to their own selves. All I know for sure about my church anymore is it's where my grandmother went to church, this is where my parents went to church, and this is where I'm going to go to church until my dying day. Unless they force me to teach VBS again. Then I might have to look into some other churches. Don't mean to be negative. I'm just sayin' an old woman is allowed to set limits.

I like our new little preacher and his pretty wife who is smart enough to smile a lot and keep her mouth shut. He's trying real hard to get our church headed in a direction other than the one we've been going which means losing a few members every year and not getting anyone new to replace them. Used to be that a person could hardly find a seat in that building. Now there's all kinds of room to spread out. Shoot, everybody there could probably lay down on a pew, stretch out, and take a nap during Sunday morning sermon and we'd have room left over.

I think Reverend Jimmy Bell might be more of the Baptist persuasion, but he ain't admitted to it yet. It's just that he has this radical belief that Christianity should involve more than sitting in a pew for an hour each Sunday, which makes a lot of us at that church a tad uncomfortable if we would admit to it. Reverend Bell seems to think that we should be out doing good deeds and telling people about Jesus all the time. Which is fine and dandy except I got a small problem with getting aggressive about telling people about Jesus here in my home town all of a sudden.

I know my neighbors real well and they know me. They know I read a chapter in my Bible every day, and they know they can count on me to pray for a sick relative of theirs if they ask me to. They know I always tell the truth even if it hurts.

I've been known to give a cashier back extra change if she makes a mistake, and I'm good for a pot of potato soup every now and then if someone's sick. I don't drink, smoke, chew or cuss....except for that one time when I was trying to cut off a rattlesnake's head with a hoe, barefoot and scared. I confess— there were a few cuss words slipped out that day. I was scared half to death.

I pay my taxes and don't cause anyone any trouble. If people around here don't know I'm a Christian by now, they ain't paying attention. If I were to suddenly start spouting off about people needing to come to Jesus everyone would start looking at me funny and wondering what had gotten into old Doreen.

Anyway, that's the reason I agreed to go help cook for that bunch of kids at the Slippery Slope Youth Camp. Reverend Jimmy Bell guilt-tripped me into it. It's all his fault.

I am a tolerable good cook and I was evidently going to have to do something more noticeable to keep up my reputation as a good Christian if I was to keep attending the Little Faith Community Church. I didn't think my nerves could take rocking crying babies or walking around South Shore knocking on doors with a handful of gospel tracts, so I said yes, and that was where I made my mistake. I shoulda asked where the camp was first. I just naturally thought it was some place fairly local. Like over in Eastern Kentucky. I thought it would at least be within the state.

It was only after I agreed to do it that the preacher told me the Slippery Slope Youth Camp was way up in Ontario, Canada. It sat on the tip end of a wilderness peninsula, stuck out in the middle of a big lake, in the middle of a big old island sitting smack dab in the middle of Lake Huron.

The church that's been trying to keep it going is even smaller than ours now, and a friend of Reverend Jimmy was the volunteer manager of it, and was overwhelmed with trying to keep it going on nothing much more than a shoe string. Reverend Jimmy and his friend thought it would be a good idea for us to take some of our menfolk and teenage boys and some tools and supplies and help spiff the place up. A lot of poor kids go to that camp, and he said it was a good project for our people to get involved in.

Jimmy asked if I had a passport. I told him no. I never needed one before. Who would have ever thought I would become a world traveler at my age! He told me I'd have to hurry up and get one. I asked him if I'd have to have shots. He choked back a laugh and said I didn't need shots to go to Canada.

Well, who knew? Ella went on a tour to the Holy Land once and she had to get shots. I figured Canada weren't no better than the Holy Land. Reverend Bell having to choke back a laugh because of my ignorance kinda hurt my feelings and I had to hold back tears. Canada is an awful long way away. What had I gone and gotten myself into?

There's not a lot I got to be proud of. I don't have no college degrees and never had no big, fancy jobs or anything. About the only thing of real value I have is my good name, so I've always made it a point that if I say I'm going to do something, I do it. So I figured I was going to have to go to Slippery Slope Youth Camp no matter what. Even if it meant figuring out how to get a passport.

Then my preacher let the other shoe drop, so to speak. He informed me that there is no electric or phone service on the island, that my cell phone couldn't even get reception there, and I'd have to cook on propane stoves, use an outdoor toilet, and bathe in the lake, and cook for eleven men and boys. He said that the only good way get to the camp is by motorboat and he suggested I might want to get a woman friend to go along with me to help.

What Jimmy don't know is that I don't have no cell phone, so that weren't no big never mind to me and although I'm not thrilled with the idea of going back to more primitive ways, I've put in my share of hours sitting in a outhouse hoping a copperhead wouldn't bite my backside while I'm doing my business. I've never bathed in a lake, but I used to carry a bar of soap down to the Ohio River on Saturday evenings when I was a kid and needed a good all-over scrubbing before church the next day. That was before I got my job at Selby and got indoor plumbing put in.

I figure propane is about like cooking on anything else although it's been a while since I cooked for anyone more than yours truly, except for when I went and took care of my brother and his wife when she was having that chemo.

Right then and there I decided it was time for Ella to take a vacation and go with me to Canada. Ella used to be the head cook over at the high school and knows a thing or three about cooking for big groups.

Well, to make a short story long, six weeks later me and Ella climbed aboard a church bus with a bunch of teenage boys and their fathers, and headed north. Can you imagine?

Ella brought a book to pass the time. I brought my crochet work, but it weren't long before I wanted to use my crochet hook to stab the Peters boy. He started the song, "Ninety-nine Bottles Of Beer On The Wall" which took us nearly to Columbus and just about drove me out of my mind before the trip was barely started.

There's a reason I live alone. I try to be a God-fearing woman but there are times when people just get on my last nerve and that song started rubbing me plumb raw. When the ninety-nine bottles of beer had been taken off the wall and passed around, he started singing a song I'd never heard of before but the boys behind me started snickering and saying it was by a group called Bare Naked Ladies.

I hate to be a prude but neither of them songs sound like something kids in a church bus oughta be singing. I kept expecting the boy's fathers to do something about it but, like some of the boys, most of them were wearing earphones and playing with little electronic gizmos. After about three-hundred miles into the trip, I started wishing I had me a little electronic gizmo to stick in my ears, too!

I was very nervous about going over the border. There's just something about being questioned by officials that makes a body feel guilty even if you're not. I think the fact that all of us were riding in a bus with the words Little Faith Community Church written on it helped. Either that or the border patrol weren't looking forward to climbing onto a bus where a bunch of teenage boys had been stewing in their own sweat for eight hours, not to mention the fact that we had eaten at Taco Bell a few hours earlier.

Teenage boys ain't real polite when it comes to digestive problems I discovered. In fact, most of them find the art of passing gas real hilarious. Some of them had taken off their big ole tennis shoes too, which was a mistake when it came to adding to the aroma of the bus.

Ella, who is sensitive to smells, just kept looking sicker and sicker and shooting me angry glances like it was all my fault she was involved in this mess. I was in the process of thinking teaching VBS and passing out gospel tracts weren't nothing compared to having to live through this trip....just about the time we pulled into the Chi-chi-maun ferry boat at the tip end of the Tobermory peninsula and me and Ella got to leave the bus and go sit in the fresh air for a couple hours.

All good things come to an end eventually and it weren't long before we had to climb back onto that bus again. Then another hour to get to the camp. All in all, it took us a full eighteen hours of bus-riding before we were looking at the dock where a boat would take us to the camp.

By the time I got down out of that church bus I was sore as a boil. Could hardly get these old legs to work. Would have been tempted to turn around and go back home except I couldn't of faced making the drive. People who travel a lot just mystify me. Give me a house with a porch any day of the week. I can see enough of life walking and driving past my little home in South Shore to satisfy me good enough.

I was proud of myself for one thing, though. I managed to get through the whole ordeal without thumping that Peterson boy on the head. He's just like his granddaddy. I used to want to thump him on the head, too, back when we were in school together.

We were met at a little dock by a man named Denny who was dad to some kids who went to that camp each summer. He had a cottage on the lake, and he said he was the volunteer bookkeeper and grounds keeper and camp manager since he lived so close. He was the kind of man who could have used a little more hair on top of his head. Especially with as cold as Canada is supposed to get in the winter time. I ain't fond of the fashion some men have of shaving their head when they think they're starting to go a little bald. Hang onto what you got as long as you can is my theory, but I suppose shaving their head cuts down on the cost of haircuts.

He looked to me like he was maybe in his late thirties, but he was wearing them low-hanging britches some young men think they got to wear to be in fashion. He weren't wearing his pants as low as I've seen some trying to do, but it was annoying enough. I don't know if the man didn't own a decent belt, or if he thought it would help him fit in with the kids who'd be coming to camp pretty soon, but it was all I could do to not tell him to act like he had good sense and pull his britches up! I was so tired and out of sorts by this time that it's a wonder I didn't say something to hurt his feelings—but Ella knows me real well, and when I drew a breath and opened my mouth, she stuck her hand over it, shook her head, and I shut up. I'll admit it. Ella's a better person than me. Has been since we was in first grade together.

So—we got into a couple little motor boats and went skimming off across the lake to the tip of this little peninsula called Slippery Slope with poor Ella hanging on for dear life.

Some people think the camp got that name because of some immoral things going on there, but Denny told us on the way over in the boat that it was named after a deep spring way back in the woods where the bank was steep and the moss around the spring was always slick with water and animals would sometimes accidentally slide down the mossy slope trying to get a drink.

Of course, after everything that happened at that camp while me and Ella were cooking there, I think maybe the name fits for things other than a spring in the woods!

Now, getting into the boat from the dock was a bit of a trick for me and Ella, but I have to admit, them boys were real chivalrous and helped us step into and out of them two little boats like we was their own grandma's. I guess it was finally dawning on them now that they'd seen the place and how far off the beaten track it was and that me and Ella were the only things between them and a week of hunger. It ain't like there's a McDonald's handy!

Another boat took the food supplies Ella and me had bought along. They had a cookhouse that weren't too bad except for the mice who'd been living there all winter long and weren't anxious to give it up. Me and Ella did battle with mice and dirt, the boys and their daddies ate peanut-butter sandwiches we let them fix their selves, and then they got started on tearing down an old bunkhouse while Mr. Droopy Drawers got the old generator started that would bring water up from the lake.

Well, we finally got ourselves sorted out. Me and Ella got us a pot of stew simmering, then we went and got all the dead spiders and flies swept out of the old cabin we'd be sleeping in. The Peterson boy brought us a bouquet of wildflowers for our room from the baseball field they were mowing, and that was so sweet of him that I decided he was a pretty good kid after all as long as he weren't singing about bottles of beer on the wall. He can't help it if he took after his grandpa. Poor thing.

We caught us four mice that first night. Ella was real proud of that. Of course, we only had four mousetraps at the camp or there would probably have been more.

Denny brought some building supplies over and everyone figured out what they were supposed to be doing and life got into a routine. I'm not usually all that excited about cooking, but them boys and their daddys was so hungry when they came in for meals that all we heard were praise and compliments. I started looking forward to setting the food out and watching them gobble it up. I even got a few hugs for doing such a good job. Of course, Ella knows her way around a three-pound slab of hamburger better than most so she's the one that needs the credit.

Denny didn't come by all that much, which was understandable since he had kids and a pregnant wife back home. After all, he was just a volunteer. Nobody could expect him to be there all the time. Besides, he owned a lumber mill somewhere on the island that he ran the rest of the time.

At least he didn't come by much until a woman showed up who introduced herself as the camp nurse. She'd come out early she said, because we were there and one of the boys might get hurt. She was a pretty thing who liked wearing short shorts. Of course the sight of them bare legs was a bit distracting to our teenage boys. I saw the Peterson boy run smack into a tree once when she was walking past.

The thing that caught me and Ella's interest, though, was how Denny started coming around a whole lot more after that pretty little nurse showed up. Turns out they'd known each other in high school and they had all kinds of things to catch up on. They sat out on the porch a'laughin' and talkin' for hours.

I suppose it was all innocent enough. They didn't go off alone or anything. It stood to reason that they'd have things to talk about. Besides, we were just two old women and it weren't none of our business anyway what they did, but I did start feeling real sorry for that pregnant wife of his. Them short shorts worried me some, too. No good thing comes out of women a'showin' themselves off like that. Especially the ones who look good while they're a'doing it. The rest of us it don't particularly matter, I suppose.

Of course me and Ella had plenty to do to keep us busy. Especially after Denny told us that one of the board members was coming for a visit. He said this was a board member who actually had some money and could help the camp if he was so minded. He asked us to make sure the kitchen was clean and a nice meal fixed. Getting company like that made me and Ella a little nervous. We started scrubbing that old kitchen like it was actually possible to get raw wood and stoves clean that had fifty years of grease baked on everything. We caught us seven more mice all told. It's hard to ever feel like a kitchen is truly clean when you got mice scurrying around.

Anyway, it turned out that the board member weren't there for a meal after all—even though Ella had outdone herself.

Mr. Haney asked Denny to unlock the camp office. I saw him in there turning pages on some ledgers and not looking very happy about what he was seeing. The nurse tried to be friendly, but Mr. Haney only seemed to have eyes for the camp financial figures. She told Ella she was going back home to Toronto for a while.

While the board member was there, Denny got real motivated and started helping our guys out. We discovered that he was pretty good with a chainsaw, hammer, and weed eater. Then at one point, we saw Mr. Haney wagging his finger under Denny's nose. We couldn't hear what he was saying but one of them ledger books was under his arm, and he opened it up and started pointing things out to Denny that Denny didn't seem none too happy to see. I figure maybe Mr. Droopy Drawers had been putting a little money in his own pocket he was not supposed to—I mean, he had all them children and he didn't seem to be spending too much time at his lumber mill or was even all that work brickle. Ella and me talked it over, and she said she thought if there was any problems with the book keeping, though, it was probably just poor math skills on someone's part. She didn't think anyone who was a Christian would take money from a church camp. She tends to cut people a little more slack than me. Maybe it's just because she's nicer. I figure people can surprise you. Sometimes it's a good surprise. Sometimes there's a lot more bad surprises inside of them than you'd ever think.

Anyways, me and Ella were watching everything out the window while we were fixing food. It was as good as watching a picture show. One thing that had worried me about coming up here was knowing I wouldn't get to watch my soap operas for a week, but now I started feeling like maybe I wasn't missing a thing. We had our own soap opera going on right under our noses. The only thing I wished was that somebody would turn up the volume!

Well, Mr. Haney took off in a motor boat and Denny slowed way down on his working around the camp until it fizzled out completely. Then he just sat there on the porch looking all sad and pouty-faced. Ella, bless her heart, wanted to cheer him up, so she decided to show off a little bit and concoct a special eight-layer cake with homemade icing and some wild strawberries on top that the boys found in the overgrown baseball field. We got so caught up in that project we lost track of Denny. The boys were happy with the eight-layer cake, though. There weren't a crumb left. We ended up not seeing Denny again for the next couple of days.

It ain't all that hot in June in Canada, but a body still works up a sweat when you're working in a kitchen over a cook stove. Me and Ella heated up a little kettle of water every morning and took a quick sponge bath before heading into the kitchen, but after a few days of that, my body started craving a good soak.

Every afternoon, Reverend Jimmy Bell and all the other fellows jumped in that lake and gave their selves a good washing before coming to the cookhouse. They always looked so refreshed after their late afternoon plunge into the lake that I started thinking it might be a good idea for me and Ella to go jump in, too. When the boys weren't around, of course. I didn't want to scare them to death with the sight of me in a bathing suit. The Peterson boy wouldn't run into a tree if he saw me walking past in my old bathing suit—he'd probably shoot himself!

The nice thing about that swimming place was that it was far, far down a path and just as private as it could be. No one but God, Himself, to watch us—and I figured that if He made us, he weren't going to be too shocked at the sight of a couple of old ladies whose bodies had seen better days.

Ella weren't too keen on the idea. She said for me to go ahead without her. I'd forgotten about Ella's fear of the water. She was okay on a boat with a life jacket on, but she said that actually getting in and swimming would scare the daylights out of her. She said she was going to stay in her cabin and put her feet up and get some shut-eye before starting supper.

So, on Thursday about noon, I got into my old polka-dot one piece, grabbed a dry towel and some shampoo and headed through the woods to where I had heard the men and boys whooping and hollering and having fun each day.

It was a long hike back through the woods and I was keeping my eye out for any snakes on the path, but I was also appreciating all the beauty around me. Them white birch trees and ferns were something special. I did think I seen a snake for a second, but it only turned out to be one of the nurse's green flip-flops I'd seen her wearing. The toe thing was made out of plastic that looked like snake skin. I remembered seeing it on her feet because I thought it was something you'd never catch me buying. I picked it up, planning to give it back to her next time she came around.

To my surprise, there was a nice floating deck to walk out on and a ladder to climb down into the water from. I laid my shampoo and soap and towel on the deck and lowered myself into that water. It was so cold it took my breath away and made me wonder if I'd gone and lost my mind.

However, I do have a stubborn streak in me, and I figured if the men and boys could take baths in this water, old Doreen could stand it, too. I've never been sure what's best when it comes to swimming in cold water—to inch into it, teeth chattering all the way, or just take the plunge and let the body get over the shock as quick as possible. I tend to lean toward the take-the-plunge philosophy. So I held my nose and threw myself off the deck frontward, swallowing up the shock of the chill of the lake, and I held my breath while my body adjusted.

My jumping-in method worked fine. In a few seconds, the water started feeling pleasant and I was able to look around and start enjoying myself. Reverend Jimmy Bell weren't kidding when he called this a wilderness camp. Here I was in this big lake ringed with nothing but trees. Everywhere I looked there was no people. Just beautiful old trees, blue sky, and blue water. I heard a loon calling in the distance and I thought, "Doreen, you're as close to paradise right now as you're ever going to get this side of heaven."

I don't care what age you are, when you get in neck-deep water, you start feeling like a kid again. I had been a strong swimmer in my youth and it all came back to me as I cavorted in that lake. Yeah, I said, cavorted. It would have looked ridiculous to anyone if they'd been looking on. I floated on my back for a while and paddled myself around with my feet, and then I did some underwater summersaults, and this old lady had about as much fun as a person can have when they're on the other side of seventy. I shampooed my hair, rinsed it out by floating on my back, and talked to a little-bitty lizard who was sunning itself and looking at me like I was the most peculiar thing it had even seen in its short life.

Since there was no one around to think I'd completely lost my mind, except the lizard and a bird or two, I even had an out-loud talk with God. I complimented him on his good work a'making this pretty lake and thanked him for shoving me out of my rut, and I even thanked him for us having the good luck to have a preacher who knew which end of a hammer to use. I've noticed that preachers who know how to work with their hands just naturally have a better attitude in general than the ones who think they gotta call a deacon to change a light bulb in their house.

Don't laugh. It's happened. I know because my daddy was the deacon that one preacher called for that very thing. Daddy told Mama that particular day that it might be a good idea for Asbury Theological Seminary down near Lexington, Kentucky to add a basic home-maintenance course to their classes.

Anyway, the lake was calm, the loons were calling to each other, and I was just floating on my back in the water with my eyes closed, feeling real good about myself, when I bumped into something. I thought it was a log, but it weren't no log. It was some man, lying face down in the water, deader than a door nail.

There are times when you discover that you are capable of a whole lot more than you ever thought. That was me at that instant. I didn't quite walk on water but I came close a'trying to get out of there! Once I hit land, I found out that I can still run pretty good, too! Hadn't run for years, but there I was high-stepping it through the ferns at triple-time getting back to camp. I didn't even take the time to watch out for snakes because I decided the snakes could watch out for their own selves. Thank goodness I'd kept my old canvas tennis shoes on in the water, or my feet would have been in bad shape the next day.

So here I come, streaking into camp, my gray wet hair flying, wearing nothing but my faded out blue polka-dot bathing suit and a pair of worn-out Keds, screeching fit to beat the band.

Charlie, the Peterson's boy's father, finally got hold of me and give me a shake. "Doreen," he said. "What on earth are you yowling about? Get your breath and tell us. Was it a snake?"

"Ain't." I bent over, put my hands on my knees, and started sucking in air trying to catch my breath. "No. Snake. Dead. Body." I pointed at the lake.

"You've got to be kidding," he said, astonished. "Another dead body?"

I nodded and caught a couple other quick gasps.

"It just don't pay to travel, Charlie," I said. "It don't pay at all! I never once found a dead body until I left South Shore."

The fellows left me standing there, bent over, wheezing, and took off like a herd of buffaloes to the swimming area. Even the boys. None of them had ever discovered a dead body before and I guess they were curious.

Me? The minute I caught my breath, my stomach decided it was its turn to act up and I had to throw up awhile. Then the shock of everything gave me a sudden case of the trots and I just managed to get to the outhouse in time. Sat there shivering and crying and just a mess. Truth be told, I was glad all the men and boys had left me stranded. It would have been plumb embarrassing if one of 'em had stayed behind to try to help me.

I managed to get myself to my cabin, stripped off my old, wet, bathing suit, got my flannel nightie on, and climbed into bed. I didn't exactly pull the covers over my head, but I came a one of doing it. I just wanted to shut out the world. Ella was up at the kitchen putting supper together by then and I figured she'd just have to take care of things without me. I weren't up to no cooking. I weren't up to nothing at all. I just lay there hoping the trots didn't start up again.

When they didn't, I calmed down and started putting my mind to work wondering who it was I bumped into out there in that lake.

The only thing I knew for sure was that I wanted to go back home to my little house. It really, really don't pay to travel far, far from home.

Soon, Reverend Jimmy Bell came back from the lake. He came a'knockin at my door and he had Ella with him. Supper got put on the back burner that night. Everyone was upset about what they'd found in the lake, and they was worried about me. Frankly, I was kinda worried about my own self.

Then Jimmy Bell told me that the dead body was Denny. Mr. Droopy Drawers himself! And him with five kids and a pregnant wife at home!

I didn't like the man, but I didn't want him dead. That shock brought on another bout of vomiting and trots. The Reverend high-tailed it out of there to get away from me and I was glad he did. I didn't want to be that sick in front of some man even if he is my preacher, but Ella stayed with me and I didn't mind that so much. She's a comforting soul. We've been best friends since we were girls and the nice thing about being around Ella is when she looks at me or when I look at her, we still see the girls we used to be—in spite of the battle scars life tends to throw at you.

The boys and their dads had cereal for supper and it didn't hurt 'em one bit.

Police came, or whatever it is they're called in Canada. Hard to tell what kinda name they use for police in a country that gives its pocket-change nicknames like Looney and Tooney and colors its paper money everything in the rainbow, like it was Monopoly money. Anyway, I had to talk to them cops. They spoke to me real careful, like I might be slow in the head. I realized after they left that I probably looked like a crazy lady with my hair all every which way, wearing my flannel nightie with the faded purple Irises. I hope I sounded like I had more sense than I must've looked like.

They wanted to know where, when, and how exactly I had found the body. After I'd answered all their questions, they went at me again asking the same ones. Well I knew what that was all about. I watch TV. I knew they thought I might trip up on some detail. I didn't think anyone could actually suspect an old woman like me of murder, but I guess they see all kinds of people and after a while they start becoming suspicious of everyone.

Me? I just felt guilty because I hadn't actually liked Denny much and now he was dead. It weren't fair of me to dislike a person just because he wore his britches a little low for a grown man, or because he sat on the porch and talked a little longer than he oughta with the camp nurse. I'm a better Christian than that, truly I am, but sometimes I forget myself and think things that just aren't all that kindly.

The police were real interested in the fact that me and Ella saw Mr. Haney a'waving his finger under the camp manager's nose the day before. Reverend Bell told us later that they went and got Mr. Haney and brought him in to the local police office for questioning, too.

When we went to bed that night I was awful grateful to have Ella there in her bunk beside mine. We left a kerosene lamp burning all night long. Maybe it was wasteful, but I just couldn't take sleeping in complete darkness that night.

A body forgets how dark it can get in the woods with no electric lights. Especially when it's overcast and you can't see the moon or stars. Especially when there is a killer on the loose. It could have been anybody. Even one of the men who came with us. Or one of the big boys we brought along. One thing for sure, though, at least that killer weren't Ella. I'd stake my life on Ella not being capable of murder.

Unfortunately, our cabin sat just a few feet from the lake and there was that steady sound of the lake all night long. It went lap, lap, lap. And every now and then one of them loons would give out one of their lonesome, reedy calls, and all I could think about was that body floatin' silently there beside me while I was swimming and splashing around thinking I was one with nature--like I didn't have good sense. There's only one way a person can truly be one with nature as far as I could

see. To be dead and buried. That's how you become one with
nature and I weren't anxious to do it.

I felt like I was nothing but a darned old fool. My biggest
fear, though, was that no one would want to be my friend
anymore since I seemed to keep finding dead bodies everywhere
I go.

The next day, we had a meeting at breakfast and Reverend
Jimmy Bell led us in prayer for wisdom to know what to do.
None of us had much of a heart for working anymore. Denny
hadn't been as work brickle as I would have liked but he
did kinda organize things and bring in supplies. I'd heard his
motorboat coming across the lake so often bringing stuff we
needed that I had gotten to where I didn't notice it all that
much. It was just a cheerful sound that blended in with all the
other nice sounds around us.

Now, the whole little island suddenly felt ominous, which
was a shame because it was such a pretty place.

Then, to make things even worse, it began to rain. And rain.
The fellows played cards in the kitchen and kept us company.
None of us much wanted to be alone right now. Ella got her
book out again and started to read. I got out my crochet work.
I didn't feel like poking anyone with the needle anymore. In
fact, I think I would have liked it if the Peterson boy had
started up the beer bottle song again. Thinking back on that
trip up there and how cheerful the boys had been, made me
long for the good old days, five days earlier, when I hadn't yet
found a dead body floating in my bath water.

There weren't no T.V. to take our minds off things. And
there weren't no radio to cheer us up neither. We just sat there
in that camp dining room, listening to the rain hitting the tin
roof, and the boys slapping down cards. Not gambling, mind
you. Reverend Bell wouldn't hear of that. (I think I told you I

suspect him of having Baptist tendencies.) They just played any old kind of card game to pass the time.

I had never been so depressed in my life, but it was helpful to know everyone else was feeling about the same way. There we were, stuck on that island, not real sure what to do, and thinking there might be a murderer on that island with us. Our reservation for the Chi-Chi-Maun weren't scheduled until the day after tomorrow so we couldn't just up and leave.

I kept thinking about everything that had happened, trying to put something together in my head that made sense. Nothing did. I started going over everything in greater detail. Was there something I missed? Some little something that might shed some light on things?

The police motored out again. They didn't know much more than when they started. Denny had been killed by a blunt object, they said. A blow to the head. I felt so sorry for his pregnant wife and them little kids of his.

Maybe he'd just had a bad fall somehow and ended up out there in the water, I suggested to the police. Maybe his shoes had been too slick.

He weren't wearing any shoes, they said.

Shoes. There was something about shoes...

That's when I remembered that one flip flop I'd found—the one that looked like it was made out of plastic snakeskin. I'd just tossed it into a bin they kept there at the swimming area for beach balls and floaty things before I went in the water. One plastic flip flop didn't amount to much in the scheme of things except for one thing—it was where I'd found it. In the middle of the path. Just the one. It weren't as though the nurse would have accidentally lost it and not realized it. No one walks along with just one flip-flop.

I didn't know if it could be significant, but I told them about it. They asked me to come show them where I'd found it on the path, and I did, even though it was still raining. I remembered where it was because after picking it up, I looked up and saw the blue lake peeking at me through the trees. It had been close to the swimming dock. I hadn't carried that flip-flop very far.

It turns out that the police had another problem. The nurse had family who lived nearby and they were starting to wonder where she was. We hadn't wondered because we thought she was in Toronto. That's where she said she was fixing to go to. Then we started all talking among ourselves and no one could remember taking her in one of the boats to the dock on the other side of the lake. There were only two motor boats, and she wouldn't have taken one by herself and left it over there or we would have noticed. It was too far to swim unless someone was awful anxious for exercise and a strong swimmer. In all the excitement, we'd done gone and lost track of the camp nurse.

The police had already looked in all the cabins, to make sure there weren't nothing amiss or anyone hiding out in one, but me and Ella hadn't looked yet. Now, we took a gander inside the cabin the nurse had stayed in, and we was surprised to find out that she'd left everything behind. Everything. The cabin had clothes, bedroll, makeup--the whole works. Of course she might have left things there deliberate except for one thing.... something we didn't know about but the police did. She'd left her medication there and Ella found it and gave it to the police.

They didn't tell us what the medicine was for, but Ella knew. She'd had a niece who'd had to take it for a while she told me—but she was ashamed when she did. The medicine was for one of them new social diseases that we never heard tell of back when we were kids.

I suppose it weren't too unusual for a single woman to have a social disease in this day and age, but it was unusual for one to leave her medication behind and not come back for it. Or her cell phone. Or her purse.

Things weren't adding up.

The rain had let up by then, and the police engaged our boys and men in doing a thorough sweep of the Slippery Slope peninsula--looking for anything that might tie in with the missing nurse. I did not participate. I stayed in my cabin. The way things were going for me, if there was anything to find, I'd be the one to find it. I'd made enough discoveries for one old woman in one lifetime. If there was something else out there to be found, I didn't think my heart could take it.

Reverend Jimmy Bell was the one who saw it first, the shallow grave among the ferns. The dead woman was in it. People don't slip and fall and hit their head and then dig themselves a grave. It was ruled a double homicide and before long our little peninsula camp was crawling with more police than I would have figured a nice, quiet place like Canada ever needed.

All work stopped, of course. Except for me and Ella. We ended up being the designated coffee brewers and sandwich makers. Reverend Jimmy Bell motored across the lake to go to the grocery store to get us some more bread and peanut butter, bless him.

The police finally found the murder weapon—it was nothing more than a croquet mallet taken from the athletic supply shack. I don't know why there was a croquet mallet there since there weren't hardly anyplace smooth enough to set up a croquet game, but I figured maybe it was donated by somebody who didn't know any better.

The croquet mallet had blood and fingerprints on it. The fingerprints weren't in the system, so we all had to be fingerprinted. They hurried up the matching process since we needed to leave the country soon—and we all got ruled out as the murderer thank goodness. Mr.Haney got released, even though he didn't have any alibi for that night except he was at home alone watching a movie on the television and going over the camp books more carefully. He'd found several thousand dollars had been skimmed off the donations. This kinda made sense to me and explained the fact that the camp was in such bad repair. But why had Mr. Droopy Drawers done such a stupid thing?

We found out the answer a few hours before we were supposed to leave to get on the Chi-Chi-Maun. Denny and the nurse had done a whole lot more than chat with each other on the front porch, as it turned out. They'd started an affair the summer before, and had kept it up. He'd started skimming money from the camp fund and squirreling it away because they was planning to run away together in a few more months.

That plan had been ruined when Mr. Haney began to suspect about the money.

Unfortunately, Droopy Drawers' wife had been suspicious ever since two days before when during her pregnancy checkup, she'd found herself with a certain disease and knew she hadn't been the one doing the running around.

Pregnancy hormones can do strange things to a woman. It can make even a sweet-tempered girl awful angry, and evidently it can turn an angry woman into a murderer. Droopy Drawers had told her he needed to stay at the camp that night, and she suspected something was going on, so she got a babysitter and followed him. She was an island girl and knew her way around a canoe, which can be real silent in the right hands. Turns out she was a big girl, too, and strong from toting them five kids around. What with the adrenaline that anger gives a person, she was able to drag little Miss Short-Shorts' body into the woods and cover it up with the loose earth you can always find in an old forest.

Instead of the little romantic get-together with his girlfriend he'd had planned, Droopy-Drawers met the end of a croquet mallet wielded by an angry wife.

Sometimes I'm real glad I ain't never been married.

So now the grandma has the five kids to raise and the pregnant wife is sitting in jail, and Miss Short-Shorts...well, no one's walking into trees over her anymore.

It's all just a crying shame, is what I think.

I'm surely glad to be home. From what I can see, a lot of people are pretty much as crazy as them loons I spent a week listening to that week I was foolish enough to get on a church bus and drive all the way to Canada.

I better get this finished. The Peterson boy is coming over soon to mow my yard for me. He don't have no grandma no more and he's kinda taken a shine to me. I'm planning on baking some cookies for him. It won't hurt me none, and it'll make him feel special. Everybody needs a grandma to fuss over them every now and then.

It feels good to do something normal like bake cookies and get my yard mowed.

I'll tell you one thing I know for sure. I ain't planning to leave South Shore, Kentucky ever again. I don't know if it's me or just sheer bad luck, but terrible things seem to happen to people when Doreen Sizemore leaves town.

Oh. And for your information, I burnt that old bathing suit. I've swum enough for one lifetime. This last time in the water just about killed me. Nope. I don't have no desire left to go splashing around in a bunch of water again. Can't tell what you might find.

Murder on the Mississippi Queen

Cousins can get a body into a whole peck of trouble if you let 'em, and that Lula Faye went and got me into an awful mess. I wish I'd never laid eyes on the woman. It's true. Even if we did grow up together and share the same bed as kids more times as not.

My name is Doreen Sizemore and I turned seventy-two years old last month. Kinda hard to believe, but there it is. I remember my mama when she turned seventy standing in front of a mirror and saying, "What is this sixteen-year-old girl a'doin in that old woman's body."

I thought it was sort of funny at the time. Now I don't. That's just how I feel sometimes if I don't do something quick to take my mind off my own self.

Now what was it I was fixing to tell?

Oh yes, Lula Faye and the mess she got me into. That woman don't have the brains of a goose.

The biggest problem with me is I have trouble saying "no" to people who need me, especially if they're kin. My mama taught me that rule. She said a person has to help kinfolks no matter what. Then there's all that guilt-producing Sunday preaching I've heard my whole life about helping others.

This is a little hard to explain, so I'll begin at the beginning and work my way up to explaining why this God-fearing, Sunday-School-going, senior citizen ended up sitting here in this little jail cell in Natchez, Mississippi, when I should have been watching my soaps at home with my feet propped up sipping a nice glass of sweet tea and waiting for my soup beans to finish simmering on the stove for dinner.

Matter-of-fact, I'd like me some soup beans right now, with a nice hunk of ham bone in 'em and a crumbly piece of buttery cornbread with honey drizzled over it. Jail food ain't all that good which probably shouldn't come as a surprise to nobody.

Now what was I talking about? Oh yes, how I ended up in jail. I'm sorry, but I'm just a little rattled. I keep thinking about what people back home in South Shore, Kentucky are going to think about me becoming a jail bird? I'll probably never live it down.

There's been times in the past when I looked at my little house in South Shore and I'd think about how I'd kinda like me a new house. Maybe one where the roof was straight across instead of sagging in the middle. Sometimes I've looked at my house and thought maybe I oughta paint it a different color or have the porch replaced or I'd wish that I could afford me some new furniture. There've been times when I'd look at my old Frigidaire and think it might be nice to have a new one that didn't make so much noise, or wish I had me one of them automatic dish washers instead of having to wash up everything my own self by hand.

I'm not thinking that way now, though. I'm so homesick for that little house of mine I don't think I'll ever want another thing if I can just get back there. A jail cell ain't no place for a seventy-two-year-old Kentucky woman who ain't never done nothing she were all that ashamed of.

If it weren't for Lula Faye's carrying's on, that's where I'd be right now. Back home without a worry in the world.

Instead, here's what happened.

I got a lot of cousins on the Sizemore side of the family. That's because my daddy's people tend to be a breedin' bunch. I have found this branch of cousins to be a mixed bag of blessings. Some are as close to me as a brother or sister and I want them to be because they're just naturally good people.

Some of my cousins are as rotten as old potatoes—the kind you find stinking up the pantry when you go sniffing around trying to figure out what smells so bad. I stay away from 'em if I can. They will either eat you out of house and home or be all nicey-nice and kissy-face when they come to visit. Then just when you're feeling all warm and toasty from the visit and said your good-byes, you find out something's gone missing-- like that pretty silver sugar spoon of my mama's that Cecelia slipped into her panty hose last time she come asking me for money, or that hunting rifle of Daddy's that Jimmy Beam Sizemore stole after asking to use the indoor toilet. (I thought he was walking awful stiff-legged when he came back out into the living room!)

There's a whole mess of Sizemore relatives I barely know way out in Salt Lake City, Utah, too. They ended up out there when my great-grandpa's oldest brother up and decided to move way out west. The rumor is that he left a girl pregnant back here he didn't want to marry but I can't prove it and its ancient history anyway. I've only seen them Utah cousins a couple of times when they come around asking questions about our family. Them people do seem plumb starved for genealogical information and I don't know why.

I got distant cousins in Congress, cousins who are priests

in the Mormon Tabernacle, and cousins who are cooling their heels in the Southern Ohio Correctional Institution.

And then there's Lula Faye Hall.

I hardly know what to say about Lula Faye. The woman defies description, but I'll try.

Here's the thing. Lula Faye's the best Baptist I've ever known. That woman plays the organ at her church and about half the time she's nodding at the choir, leading it by bobbing her head with the music at the same time. She teaches Sunday school, Vacation Bible School, Children's Church, is in charge of two visitation committees (one for the physically ill, and one for the wayward sinners) and she volunteers part-time as a church secretary whenever Marva, the real church secretary, gets sick.

Marva told me once that it ain't smart for her to get sick very often. She's afraid that if she's out of the office for any length of time, Lula Faye will talk the deacons into giving her the job.

Lula Faye is like that. She can talk people into doing just about anything. It ain't that she's hard-hearted. She's not. It's just that she thinks she knows what's best for everybody and believes that her opinions are the exact same ones as the Lord's.

I heard a preacher say once that Lula Faye was often wrong but never uncertain. That described her real good, but that preacher didn't last long at that church.

She's the kind of woman who is always going on about the Lord telling her things. For instance, last summer she said the Lord had told her that I should make ten dozen cookies for her church's Vacation Bible School that year. I told her that was right odd because the Lord hadn't said anything to me about baking no ten dozen cookies for her church's VBS.

Of course, I made the cookies for her anyway but she didn't have to bring the Lord into it to get me to do it. Like I said,

I was taught to help people out and I'm pretty certain He has bigger issues to deal with than whether or not I bake Lula Faye some cookies.

Basically, Lula Faye just wears me and everyone else around her plumb out. Most people learn early on that it's wise to just go ahead and do whatever Lula Faye wants done once she backs you up against a wall. It's easier that way and usually takes less time and energy than arguing with her.

Sometimes I pity her preacher. Whoever he happens to be at the time. That church can't seem to keep hold of a preacher for more than a year or two and I have a good idea why. I know for a fact that last Easter she sat down and wrote a sermon she wanted her preacher to preach. She even sketched out on paper suggestions she had for hand gestures. I about swallowed my teeth when she showed it to me. That preacher left a week later. Just picked up and moved his whole family out of state. Lula Faye couldn't figure out why he would do such a thing when she'd tried to be so helpful.

I've heard rumors that word has even gotten out in the preacher schools about Lula Faye. Don't know if it's true, but I heard for a fact that the preacher selection committee at Lula Faye's church started running out of candidates who would apply for the job.

It ain't just the preachers that Lula Faye scares off, either. She likes to give the preacher's wives a few little helpful suggestions now and again. Like comments on their clothes and how they keep house, and how they raise their kids. I have an idea that might have something to do with the frequent turnover of preachers at Lula Faye's church. None of my business of course. It ain't my church and I got opinions about people who have too many opinions about other people's churches.

Basically, I think the main problem is that Lula Faye is one of them high energy people who don't have enough to do with their time.

Lula Faye had a husband for a while. His name was Earl but everyone called him Poor Stupid Earl because Lula Faye always called him that and it kinda stuck. That was a shame because Earl weren't stupid and he weren't poor. He was, however, kinda weak and Lula knew how to take advantage of a person's weakness, but only for their own good of course.

Actually, if you want the whole story, Lula Faye accidentally gave him a last name, too. Behind his back a lot of people called him "Poor-Stupid-Earl-Bless-His-Heart."

Every time I'd see her back when Earl was alive, she'd tell me something he'd done that she thought was dumb and then she'd say something along the lines of, "Oh, Doreen. That poor stupid Earl, bless his heart, went and forgot to put oil in the riding lawnmower again and it done all burnt up." Or, "That poor stupid Earl, bless his heart, done ran off the side of the road and got stuck in a ditch."

Funny thing, Earl was a smart man. One of the few men in our county who graduated from college back then which was quite an accomplishment for a boy who crawled out from these hills. Taught at Greenup High School most of his life, won some awards with his kids in the science club if I remember right. But to Lula Faye he was just poor, stupid, Earl, bless-his-heart.

In case you ain't never lived here, people who live in Kentucky know that if you say, bless his or her heart, in a certain tone of voice before saying something bad about someone it takes the sting out of the statement and don't make you sound so mean. Like you love 'em a whole lot, but they do have this one regrettable trait. Lula Faye does it with Marva, too.

"Now, Marva, bless her heart, just don't know a thing

about running off the bulletin. She uses the wrong color ink. I could do such a better job. It's just pitiful."

"Pitiful" is a word Lula Faye uses a lot, too. She also likes the word "precious." People, in Lula Faye's world are either "pitiful" or "precious." Except for Earl, who was poor and stupid.

Actually, I always liked Earl a sight better than I did Lula Faye. He was a kind man who wore an expression on his face as though he could hardly believe what he'd gotten himself into. Nobody much noticed when he passed away, though. He was that sort of person. If there hadn't been a funeral that Lula Faye was in charge of and therefore quite a show, people might not have noticed he was gone for some time. He was the kind of person you didn't notice right off. It was Lula Faye you noticed with her big voice, and loud laugh and bright red lipstick.

Now I know bright red lipstick ain't exactly a Baptist thing, but Lula Faye wore it anyway. She said she looked too washed out without it. That red lipstick might have been a sign of things to come if I'd cared enough to notice.

Anyway, Earl died way up in Huntington. He was supposed to be at some sort of miniature train conference. He liked making little train tracks in his and Lula Faye's basement. Model trains were one of the few things Lula had no interest in or opinion on so I guess when he was in his basement he felt like he had some control over his own life—more or less.

You would've thought that being widowed at the tender age of sixty-two would have caused Lula Faye to rethink her life a little. Maybe ease up on the people around her, but she stuffed her grief over Earl down deep—I think she really did love the man—pasted a smile on her face, and kept on doing what she'd been doing most of her life which was bossing everyone around who came near her.

Then the preacher selection committee found one more preacher willing to come to our neck of the woods and the committee people weren't real particular by this time. Roy Abernathy did not have a seminary education or even a high school education. What he had was a GED. He knew his Bible, though and was willing to work for the small salary they was offering--which is what the committee must have decided is what really counts in a preacher.

Roy was rough as a cob to look at and nearly as opinionated as Lula Faye. We found out later that he'd spent the first half of his adult life in prison where a chaplain got hold of him and turned him around. I've never known a preacher who got his Bible education while sitting in a prison cell, but I guess he must've had plenty of time to study it. The man could quote long passages from the Bible at the drop of a hat.

He came to that church craggy-faced and solemn and without any of the inconvenient baggage most preachers carry around with them—like a wife and kids. Best of all, he weren't scared of Lula Faye. He weren't even impressed by her. I guess when a man has survived years of incarceration with murderers and thieves a bossy woman ain't nothin' to worry about. I'm pretty sure his lack of being scared of Lula Faye was one of the things that endeared him to the rest of the church. I'll just be flat-out honest here. That Lula Faye could be a bully, bless her heart.

I'll tell you a funny about him and her. He'd only been there a week or two and Lula Faye hadn't got a handle on who she was dealing with. She had a big idea for Vacation Bible School—something she'd seen on some sort of computer video thing I think she called You Two or Tube Face or something like that—and she cornered her new preacher to tell him all the reasons why he oughta make it happen.

Me and her was having us some lunch at the little restaurant one of our local gas stations has, and Preacher Roy Abernathy came walking in to pay for his gasoline. Lula Faye jumped up and started chattering to him about what he oughta do about VBS. He paid for his gas, put his wallet back into his pocket and then he looked her square in the face and said, "No."

Just that. A simple "no."

Lula Faye weren't sure she'd heard him correctly so she told him all about it again. He waited for her to run out of breath and then he shook his head and said, "No" again. Then he walked on out of there and left Lula Faye standing in the middle of the gas station looking at the door like she couldn't believe her eyes or her ears. She weren't used to being told "no."

Of course, I was sitting there trying not to choke on my barbecue sandwich, but it was just about the funniest thing I'd ever seen. Lula Faye was quiet and pensive for the rest of the afternoon like she was trying to figure some things out.

So—back to my story—I got this phone call from Lula Faye right after I'd been to the beauty shop for my perm. She said she needed to see me right away and was I at home and could she come over?

If I hadn't been feeling pretty good about myself right then because of my fresh hairdo I probably would have turned her down. But since I was in a good mood, I thought I could handle a visit from her and told her yes, to just come on over and we'd have us a nice visit.

Since I'd already watered my garden and had been to the beauty shop and all, there weren't a whole lot for me to do to get ready. No last-minute throwing on a clean dress or anything. I even had me some fresh pickle loaf lunch meat I'd picked up at the grocery store and a new loaf of white bread and some beef steak tomatoes I'd gotten out of the garden and sliced up. The only thing left that I needed to do was make us a pitcher of sweet iced tea to wash the pickle loaf down with. I had half a carrot cake from the day before when we had a potluck at my church so I even had desert, too. Lula Faye was always a fool for any kind of cake.

So I made that sweet tea, put it in the fridge, and then went out to sit on my front porch feeling spiffy. I had on my next-to-best house dress, was fresh from the beauty shop with my new cut and perm, and had the fixings of a real nice lady-lunch all ready to go when Lula Faye came to visit. I didn't think she could find too much fault in anything, although with Lula Faye you couldn't never tell what she might find to criticize.

It weren't that she was mean, Lula Faye had a heart of gold, and if you didn't pick up on that fact right away, she'd tell you so. The problem was, Lula Faye was what some people call a perfectionist and she just had to have things perfect or at the very least point out the flaw to everyone around.

Now me, I kinda like flaws, whether they be in people or furniture or houses. I think it makes things more interesting. It's probably one of the reasons I like living here in South Shore, Kentucky which has plenty of flaws.

Perfection ain't all that interesting to me, but maybe I'm just justifying my own flaws and I got plenty of them, too. Can't help it. That's the way life is. Sometimes it can kinda beat a person up. I guess that's why I don't usually find young folk all that interesting anymore. There they are, all shiny and new and stupid with big ideas and big plans. All of 'em thinkin' they won't be like us. They won't never get old or sick or have to scrape to put two cents together. Except for that Peterson boy who comes to mow my lawn. He's starting to act like he's got good sense.

Anyway—where was I now? Oh yes, Lula Faye. As I sat there waiting, I realized that Lula Faye hadn't sounded so good to me on the phone. Kinda strangled-like. She didn't talk my ear off like usual, either. Just asked if I was home and could she come on over. All serious. Of course if I hadn't of said yes she'd have come on over anyway. That's Lula Faye's way.

One of the nice things about staying in one place and being raised up with people you've known all your life is that you usually know their mama and daddy and more often than not their grandparents too. That can help you understand why some people are the way they are.

I'd watched Lula Faye get raised up by the most nervous, high strung woman we ever had around these parts. Aunt Belle was all powder and rayon dresses and hose with seams up the back and little tiny sandwiches on a tray when you came over. She made company sandwiches out of Cheez Whiz and white bread with the crusts cut off and a little tiny sweet pickle on the side. For some reason that business of cutting off the crusts got on my mama's last nerve.

"What's wrong with crusts?" Mama would say. "Belle must think she's something on a stick, making sure she cuts off the crusts and cuts them into little squares and triangles."

"Now, Milly," my daddy would say. "She's just high strung. That's all. You got to remember, Belle's from Georgia and they do things different there. Maybe she don't know no better than to waste perfectly good bread by cutting off the crusts."

My mama didn't believe in wasting anything. She even told me when I was a little girl that if I ate the crusts off my bread I'd end up with curly hair. Mama lied about that. My hair is straight as a poker. I didn't never get curly hair until I got my job over at Selby Shoes across the Ohio River and got my first pay check. First thing I did with my first few dollars I earned all by myself was go to the beauty shop and get myself a permanent wave. Had one ever since. I just don't feel right unless my hair has some curl in it. I see old women walking around with their hair all gray and straight and flat on top of their heads and they don't look like they got good sense to me.

Now, what was I talking about?

Oh yes, Lula Faye. Turned out her mama weren't dressing up and putting on high heels and a pearlite necklace and making sure her seams were straight just because she was from Georgia. Nope. Belle had a few problems we didn't know nothing about when Uncle Jasper came back from the army already married to her and acting like he had himself a movie star actress on his arm. Proud as punch.

Me, I always thought Aunt Belle seemed a might distracted, like she was hearing music no one else heard, or thinking thoughts no one else had thought before, but that turned out not to be it. Aunt Belle had a party going on in her mind that none of us knew nothing about.

Now there I go, getting ready to tell you all about poor Aunt Belle, bless her heart, and it just wouldn't be the right thing to do. My mama always said if you can't say something nice about somebody, don't say nothing at all, and there's not a whole lot nice I can say about Aunt Belle except she pretty much spoiled Lula Faye to death.

You ever see Nellie Olson on that TV show called Little House on the Prairie? There was that bossy little girl with the blonde curls big as sausages and a bow in her hair and a big frown? That kinda describes Lula Faye growing up. Aunt Belle kept her in these frilly dresses with big bows in her hair and taught her how to sit with her legs crossed at the ankles all the time. Aunt Belle would fuss at her even when she was little and it was just us kids playing around and some women friends visiting together. My mama later said when word got out about Aunt Belle, that maybe she should have tried keeping her legs crossed at the ankles! But there I go. About to say something bad about someone instead of nice.

So something I can say nice, let me see. Well, Aunt Belle always smelled good. It was that rose-scented toilet water she wore, my mama said. My daddy made the mistake of saying that in her defense once when Mama was going on and on about all of Aunt Belle's peculiarities. Daddy said, "Well at least the woman smells good."

Mama got mad and said if she had some of that expensive imported toilet water like Uncle Jasper paid good money to get for Aunt Belle, maybe she'd smell like roses, too.

Daddy had the good sense to quit talking about that time. I was little and couldn't figure out why toilet water would be a good thing or why it would be expensive. Making water in an outdoor toilet was something I was familiar with 'cause we didn't have no indoor plumbing at home back in them days and our toilet never smelt like roses to me, so I was a little confused, except Aunt Belle's perfume was pretty loud, and sometimes made my nose and eyes water when it was fresh and she hugged me—so I thought maybe she might have gotten it from a toilet after all.

I was nearly twenty before I realized one day when I was watching some program on TV that it must have been "toilette" water they were talking about—something Frenchy and fancy—and not water you'd find in a toilet at all.

Where was I now?

Oh yes. I was trying not to say anything bad about Aunt Belle even if she did run off with the postman when Uncle Jasper's back was turned. Lula Faye was seventeen when that happened and all that time she'd thought she was the apple of her mama's eye and it turned out it was Hadley Phillips, the postman who was really the apple of Aunt Belle's eye.

Mama said she'd wondered why the mail was always so late getting to our house.

It was a shock to Lula Faye of course. And Uncle Jasper,

too, but mainly Lula Faye. I have to admit, by the time Aunt Belle run off, I was eighteen and getting a little tired of Lula Faye and her always acting like her you-know-what didn't stink so I kinda enjoyed the fact that Aunt Belle had run off. At least I enjoyed it for a couple seconds and then I got hold of myself and started feeling bad for Uncle Jasper. He was a nice man.

Problem was, other people felt sorry for Uncle Jasper, too, and some of them were of the middle-aged female persuasion. Lot of them were good cooks which came in handy since Lula Faye didn't know how to make nothing to eat except them little bitty sandwiches like her mama made. I guess Cheez Whiz sandwiches can get old after a while, even if you do cut the crusts off.

After some of the women of our town figured out that Uncle Jasper might be up for grabs and him a good upstanding man with a decent job and a heart of gold and a veteran to boot, well, let's just say them were the days of the casserole wars at Uncle Jasper's and Lula Faye's. Uncle Jasper never ate so good but Lula Faye was embarrassed out of her mind.

Uncle Jasper didn't remarry for a long time and he made a good thing of it, too. His grocery bill probably weren't nothing considering the fact that all them lonely women kept bringing him sympathy food and Uncle Jasper apparently developed a need for a whole lot of sympathy.

He was naturally upset when Aunt Belle left him, but after things calmed down Uncle Jasper looked around and saw the possibilities stretched out before him—so to speak—and developed this pitiful, sad face and soulful eyes, and started enjoying his role as the most eligible bachelor in South Shore, Kentucky.

Lula Faye was furious at him for acting like that, and the more ashamed she was of him, the better Baptist she become. That woman could run a Vacation Bible School like you never saw. There had to be five different shades of Kool-Aid for her church's kids and no store-bought cookies at her refreshment table. No sir! She personally vetted each church member's contributions to the refreshment table and if them VBS cookies looked like they might have spent time boxed up on a grocery store shelf, she'd wrinkle up her nose and push them to the side. I heard her say once, when someone new to her church handed her a plate of Nutter-Butter cookies, that maybe she'd bring them out for the children if they ran out of the "good" cookies first.

I have a suspicion that Earl might have eaten a few of them evil store-bought cookies down in his hidey-hole in the basement where he had his train track. All I know is I saw him a'sneaking them out from under the VBS table when she weren't looking, and he had a little smile on his face like he had big plans for them Nutter-Butters.

Anyways.

Where was I again? Oh yes. I think I was about to tell you how Lula Faye ended up on my doorstep a'crying that day.

Well, I was on the front porch when she drove up and got out of her car. I knew in an instant that something was bad wrong. Lula Faye didn't look so good. Her face was all splotchy, her hair was standing up in odd places, and her green shirtwaist dress was buttoned up wrong and hanging down at her knees a couple of buttons off. Of course that made the neck of her dress all wee-waw and funny looking. The woman hadn't even dressed herself properly. That had never happened before.

"What on earth is wrong, Lula Faye?" I stood up while I waited for her to climb up the porch stairs. Lula Faye in this sort of shape weren't a sitting-down matter. I was genuinely concerned.

She didn't answer me because it looked like she was too busy trying not to burst out bawling. Instead, she walked into my arms and just held onto me and started sobbing and shaking. I hadn't seen her this upset ever in my life. Not even when Poor-Stupid-Earl-Bless-His-Heart died. I couldn't begin to imagine what might have happened to cause her to fall apart like this.

Now we ain't exactly a hugging family. If anything, we tend to hold each other at arm's length most of the time—but today weren't the time to hold to that family tradition. Lula Faye was heart-broken and I was gettin' scared of what the matter was, so I wrapped my arms around my cousin and held on.

"You'll hate me," Lula Faye pulled away from me finally, wiped her eyes, and swallowed a couple of sobs. "You'll think I'm as awful as my mama."

Well, actually, I'd never thought her mama was all that awful except back when I still thought she wore perfume that she'd gotten out of an outhouse.

"Tell me what you done, Lula Faye," I said. "Just spit it out. You ain't killed nobody have you?" Then a thought struck. Maybe she was more like her mama than I'd thought. "You been a'sleeping in someone's bed you got no right to be sleeping in?"

"Of course not." She took two steps back from me and in doing so nearly fell off the porch into my pink begonias. I had to grab hold again and steady her. "I'd never do something like that. What kind of a person do you think I am?"

"I don't know." I let go of her. "You got to tell me what you did first."

"Let's go inside," she said, suddenly getting all suspicious around the eyes. "I don't want anyone else to know."

So we went inside, and she sat down on my couch and smoothed her dress down over her knees like her mama taught her way back in elementary school—although the fact that her dress was buttoned up wrong kinda spoiled the effect.

"You ever do something bad, Doreen?" she asked. "Something you'd be ashamed for other people to know?"

The sobbing was over, but she grabbed a tissue from a box beside her and started dabbing her eyes because they were still leaking.

I gave her question some thought before I answered. Had I ever done something I was ashamed of? Well, I got a quick mouth on me and I tell people off sometimes when I probably shouldn't. Sometimes I eat a few too many lemon-flavored Moon Pies when I'm feeling lonely. I don't get all gooshy-eyed over babies like some women do, and I've been known to watch a little more TV than is good for me—but bad? Really bad? I'd never seen anything I wanted to do bad enough to deal with the aggravation and consequences.

"No," I said. "I ain't done nothing all that bad. Why?"

"Well, don't judge me 'til I tell you the whole thing," Lula Faye said. "Promise?"

"I'll do the best I can not to judge," I said. "But I ain't making any promises. What did you go and do, Lula Faye? Rob a bank?"

I was starting to wish I'd gone ahead and had me a sandwich of that nice pickle loaf I'd bought. It didn't look like this was going to be the luncheon I was expecting after all and now I was getting hungry.

"I won the lottery," she sniffled.

"You what?" I weren't sure I heard her right.

"I won the lottery."

"You mean the twenty-dollar scratch off kind?"

"No, Doreen. I mean I won the whole dang thing."

Well now that give me something new to think about. Lula Faye might have had her faults, but she weren't no liar... and the lottery had been getting a lot of press lately. It had gone up and up and a lot of people had been playing it who wouldn't usually. Anyway, it must be true because I'd never heard Lula Faye say the word "dang" before in her life. It would take something powerful big for her to say that. In Lula Faye's world, that's right up there with using the real D-word.

"You what?" I really didn't know what else to day. It ain't every day that your first cousin tells you she won the lottery and uses a bad word to boot. "Are you sure?"

"I'm sure." She reached into her purse and pulled out a ticket-thingy and showed it to me. I didn't know quite what to make of it. I don't follow the lottery, so to speak.

"It's all the right numbers. I played my hunches and they were the right ones this time."

"But you're a Baptist!" I said. "I didn't think Baptists were allowed to gamble."

"I know," she wailed. "Gambling's a sin and that makes me nothing but a big fat sinner!"

Now, I know I've heard that preached my whole life, that gambling's a sin—and I'm sure if a body is going to take food out of their children's mouth or gamble off the farm, it's a sin for sure. But winning it? Was that a sin? I had no idea. I weren't no Baptist.

"How long you been playing?" I asked.

"A long time," she admitted. "I always drove to another town, though. I didn't want anybody to know. It was a bad secret I kept inside for a lot of years."

"Even when Earl was alive?" I asked.

"Poor stupid Earl never knew a thing, bless his heart, but yes—I'm ashamed to say that I did. It give me something to do while he was playing with his trains. It was kind of like I had this little secret sin that wasn't hurting anyone. I never spent a lot of money on it."

I leaned forward. This was fascinating. Maybe Lula weren't

completely the righteous pain in the neck I'd always thought she was.

"What are you going to do?" I asked.

"I don't know!" she sniffled. "If I collect the money, people will know what I done."

"I suppose it wouldn't be considered a sin if you give it all to the church."

She clutched her purse to her chest—like I was fixing to take it away from her.

"I can't do that," she said.

"Why not if you don't want it."

"I didn't say I didn't want it. And besides, I'm not going to let that jail bird preacher have it, that's for sure!"

Well, now. I guess that would pay him back for telling Lula Faye "no."

"How much did you get?" I finally thought to ask.

I weren't prepared for the answer, though. I hadn't been paying a whole lot of attention to the numbers. I might have some weaknesses of my own, but they tend to run to the moon pie variety and gambling weren't one of them.

"There aren't any other winners," Lula Faye said. A gleeful look stole over her face. "If I turn this ticket in I'm supposed to get fifty-two million dollars."

Well, you could have knocked me over with a feather. I didn't even know how to wrap my mind around such a figure.

"Fifty-two million dollars?" I asked.

She nodded. Her eyes as big as saucers like a little girl who just told somebody a big secret.

"You?"

She nodded again.

"Anybody else know about this?"

"No." She shook her head. "Not yet."

"Why are you telling me?" I asked.

"Because you're smarter than me," she said. "You always were. I figured you'd know what to do."

Well, now that's the first I ever heard her say anything like that. I'd always thought she treated me like I didn't have a brain in my head.

I live on a social security check that comes to just under eight hundred dollars a month. It's better than nothing, but it ain't anything to write home about. My little house is paid for. I know how to keep a good garden, and I don't eat much. I don't own a car. The biggest thing I pay for is my electricity bill which I try to keep under fifty dollars a month by hanging out my laundry to dry and keeping the thermostat turned way down. I buy what clothes I wear at Goodwill or sometimes at the Dollar Store if I'm hankering after something new. They got pretty good-looking clothes at the Dollar Store these days.

All thoughts of pickle loaf went plumb out of my freshly permed head. I just sat there with my teeth in my mouth, as my mama used to say when someone was too surprised to speak. Then my stomach growled and I decided even if someone has just won fifty-two million dollars, a body still has to eat.

"You want a pickle loaf sandwich?" I asked. "I got sweet tea, too."

"Maybe just a nibble," Lula Faye said. "I doubt I can hold anything down much."

Go ahead and call me a hypocrite, but I cut the crusts off them sandwiches just like Lula Faye liked when she was a little girl. I'd never done that before for her but I'd also never had a millionaire sitting with her feet under my table and her dress buttoned crooked before. I weren't real sure what the etiquette for such a situation was supposed to be.

"What are people going to think of me, Doreen?" Lula Faye said. "What are they going to be saying behind my back?"

"Does it matter?"

To tell the truth, I liked her better today than I ever had. It weren't because of the money. It was because for the first time in our lives she weren't trying to boss me around. In fact, the first words out of her mouth after she took a bite out of that pickle loaf sandwich was that my new perm looked nice.

"Seriously, Doreen." She took a big gulp of the sweet tea I'd set in front of her and reached for another sandwich. So much for that little nibble. "What are people going to think?"

"Most of 'em are going to think that you're one lucky woman winning the state lottery like that. The rest of 'em are going to hit you up for a loan the minute they see you. This area ain't exactly rolling in money."

"I know," she said. "People are gonna act weird around me when the news gets out ain't they."

"People already act weird around you," I pointed out. "It'll be okay. They'll still be happy for you."

Actually, I had my doubts. Some people can be kinda sharp when it comes to other people having good fortune. It's like they get mad it didn't happy to them.

The one thing I know about Lula Faye is that she was ashamed of her mama and embarrassed by her daddy, and she spent most of her life trying to prove to people that she was better than them. I guess she thought she had to save the reputation of the family or something all by herself. What she didn't seem to ever appreciate was the fact that people don't really care all that much what other people do or don't do. At least not any more. Not after a steady diet of some of them reality TV shows where a girl tries to figure out which one of eight possible baby daddies is the real daddy and then it turns out a couple of them baby-daddies have been sweet on the girl's mama. After watching a few of them kinds of shows, a regular person's dirty laundry just don't amount to much anymore.

Like I said, sometimes I watch a little too much TV.

Besides, Lula Faye's mama and the postman set up to housekeeping down in Frankfort and got married and acted like they had right good sense after they got the running around part out of their system. Before he died, Lula Faye's daddy was telling people that Aunt Belle leaving him was one of the best things ever happened to him. Of course, he was a lot heavier by that time, and he did die of that coronary. Probably from all the casseroles and homemade pies he was forever getting left in his fridge. From what I heard, he got to leaving his door unlocked because he didn't want to keep the food from showing up.

I always wondered why them women didn't give up after a while, but I guess they figured they'd all invested way too much Campbell's Cream of Mushroom Soup making them casseroles to stop. The way I remembered it, he outlived most of the front runners.

"So—what are you going to do?" I asked.

Lula Faye had begun to get some of her spunk back. I noticed she was sitting up a lot straighter instead of all slumped over the table. It's amazing what some sweet tea and a pickle loaf sandwich can do for a body, especially if there's someone sitting across from you who ain't judging the fact that you played the lottery. After all, everyone's got something they ain't too proud of. If they say they don't, they're lying. Even the Holy Book says that.

"What am I going to do?" She lifted her chin and crunched into a potato chip. I'd dumped a bag of them into a bowl to round the meal out. "I'm going to turn in this ticket to the lottery people, that's what I'm going to do."

"What are you going to do with the money?" I asked.

"I figure that out later," Lula Faye said. "But I got me some ideas."

The problem with winning the lottery is that you can't

keep it a secret no matter what. That means everybody and his brother knows you got money. I never thought much about it before, but when you win the kind of money that Lula Faye won, the news reporters try to find out everything they can about you.

There weren't much dirt they could dig up about Lula Faye. Of course some of the news people interviewed some local friends of hers asking what kind of a person she was. I thought I noticed a bit of hesitation from some of her church members before they told the reporters that she was a wonderful, God-fearing woman. Salt of the earth, they said. It was like it took a beat for everyone to work out in their minds that it was okay to tell maybe a little white lie in order to keep outsiders from knowing church business.

The fact was—and I knew it—that Lula Faye had been a thorn in everyone's side for a whole lot of years, and they were being awful nice in spite of it. Sometimes people can surprise you in a good way. Or maybe they thought some of Lula Faye's money might come their way if they were nice.

I was a little worried when I saw on the news that they'd manage to corner Preacher Roy Abernathy outside the church one evening when he was mulching the flower beds.

"What do you think about your parishioner winning the lottery?" The blow-dried blonde girl had a microphone in her hand and a too-serious expression on her face. "Do you expect her to give some of her winnings to the church?"

There ain't much for our local news people to work with sometimes in our neck of the woods and the local news channels were milking Lula Faye's good fortune for all it was worth.

The blonde girl stretched out her hand with the microphone to catch what Preacher Roy might say. He stood up, dusted the dirt off his knees and hands and said, "No. I don't."

"But she's a member of your church," the newsgirl argued. "Certainly the church could use a portion of her winnings."

I didn't know Preacher Roy all that well and I scooted forward in my seat to hear what the man would say.

"What Lula Faye does with her money is her own business. Not mine. And certainly not yours."

Well, the news girl kinda jerked back when he said that. She probably wished she could re-wind the tape—but the interview was live, so she felt like she had to justify herself with a follow-up question.

"But most churches have needs," she said. "Doesn't yours need a new roof or something?"

Preacher Roy glanced up at the white framed church with its pretty steeple. "This church building is a hundred and seventy years old. It survived one tornado, a fire that took part of the back end, and the Civil War. The foundation is still sound, there's no termite damage, and that roof does not leak. If it did, I would repair it myself. But if it were to burn to the ground tomorrow the church would still stand."

The young news girl was puzzled. "What do you mean?"

"The church is not a building." He picked up a rake that was leaning against the outside of the building. "The gospel has survived without lottery money for over two thousand years and it can last a few more. Now, if you'll excuse me."

He turned his back on the reporter and began to rake the mulch smooth. His craggy face had never cracked a smile the whole interview. It struck me that this was one preacher who was real serious about his faith. I was a little surprised the channel allowed that interview to stand, but there weren't much they could do about it. It being a live broadcast and all.

It made me feel like if it weren't for the fact that Lula Faye went there, and the fact that I was sort of a Methodist (now that we've become a community church, so to speak, I'm not real sure what to call myself.) I wouldn't mind hearing that man preach some time. One thing for sure, he weren't trying to win any popularity contests with that news channel. I figured that would be the last time they'd ask him for any kind of interview.

Some of the people of Lula Faye's church were thrilled for her and some of the younger people started talking about playing the lottery their own selves seeing as how Lula Faye was a rich woman now and all. Older members of the church weren't real happy about that and pointed out that gambling was a sin—even if you did win fifty-two million dollars. This hurt Lula Faye's feelings and she stopped playing the organ for them. Quite a few men started coming around and asking her out. Men who had steered clear of her before. I guess most of them thought they could put up with a little bossiness out of her if it meant getting to buy a new bass boat or fancy RV, but Lula Faye was not interested in any of them.

Then some of our relatives on the Sizemore side started coming around asking for financial help. It's amazing how the smell of money can draw people to you. Like flies to honey, Lula Faye said. She was a little put out with them.

There were also some strange letters from people. Some were so strange that Lula Faye got a company to come and put a security system in. She made the mistake of buying a fancy car, and then worried about parking it where people might hurt it. When it did get a scratch, she was pretty sure it was deliberate. People around here can be as good as gold to you when you're down and out, but there's some who can get awful mean if they think someone is getting above themselves.

At least Lula Faye didn't build herself a big new house or anything. She actually had some common sense about that. Said since it was just her, she didn't need some mansion to live in.

Of course, with Lula Faye being rich and everything, Marva, the church secretary, started to relax about hanging onto her job. She was pretty sure Lula Faye didn't want it anymore and she was right.

Lula Faye tried her best to act like nothing had changed, at least for a while she did, but the fact was things had changed. She felt funny at church, and she felt funny going to the grocery store, and she felt funny every time she tried to talk to people who knew her. She said they didn't seem to know what to say to her. Except for them who had big plans for her money. She told me that she'd never realized how many relatives she had before. Cousins were suddenly coming out of the woodwork.

Lula Faye had always been bossy, but she really did have a good heart. She had spent most of her life trying to live down what her mama did, and what her daddy had turned into, and it was like she had created a bunch of self-imposed rules to live by and the only problem she had was trying to make everyone else live by them, too. Suddenly, having her whole life turned upside down with that big bunch of money and no rule book attached to it to tell her what to do, threw her way off-kilter.

The worst thing was, Lula Faye had no earthly idea how to continue to be a good Baptist and still keep her lottery money intact. People at her church started talking about what they'd do if they were her and how Lula Faye could support mission work for an entire third world country if she wanted to.

The problem was, Lula Faye didn't want to support mission work for an entire third world country. Lula Faye decided that what she really wanted to do was have some fun for a change and that's when the real trouble began—for both of us.

She wanted someone to go have fun with her and for some reason she decided she wanted me to be her traveling partner. There's some around here who would be thrilled with the idea, but I was the worst choice she could have made.

"I've decided I got to get out of here for a while," Lula Faye said, about a month into her being a rich woman. "I need to take a vacation and clear my head, and you're coming with me, Doreen."

"Me?"

"Yes. You ain't got anything else you gotta do."

I told you before--nothing good ever comes from me leaving home. After that church camp business, I'd made a serious vow to myself that I'd never set foot outside of Greenup County, Kentucky again. Ever.

"Nope," I said. "You're gonna have to find yourself another girl. I like it here at home just fine."

"I'll pay," Lula Faye said. "It won't cost you a cent."

"Nope." I had made my decision and I crossed my arms across my chest to emphasize the fact that I felt real strong about it. I didn't want to go with her and that was that.

One of the nicer things about getting old is you know what you want to do and what you don't want to do. And I knew the one thing on earth I had no intention of ever doing was setting foot outside of my home town ever again—except for maybe going over the Ohio river to Portsmouth every now and then to see my eye doctor or shop at Walmart.

But one of the bad things about dealing with relatives is that they know your weaknesses, all of them, and Lula Faye knew mine. We'd spent too many hours sitting on the banks of the Ohio River together.

"I bet I know how to get you to go with me." Lula Faye said, in a kind of sing-song like a little girl would use.

"Ain't happening," I said.

But I was wrong and Lula Faye was right. She did know how to get me out of Greenup County. I just didn't know it yet.

There's pretty much only one thing I ever really wanted to

do that I ain't done yet. Every now and then one of them nice old paddle boats come down the river looking like some sort of fancy wedding cake and playing that big ole calliope. People stand at the boat's railing and wave at us a'sittin' there on the river bank. I'd always wished I could be one of them people waving at us and Lula Faye knew it.

Of course, I also knew that wishing to go on one of them trips down the Ohio River was about like wishing on the moon. People like me don't go making trips that costs what them riverboat cabins cost. Shoot—if I ate nothing but peanut butter and white bread for a year I couldn't afford to go on no trip like that.

The other problem was, Lula Faye had already booked us a room on the Mississippi Queen Riverboat. It was coming down the river in two days, she said, and she'd found out about it and decided to treat me to the one trip I'd longed to go on forever.

I don't know why the idea of floating down the river had always held such appeal for me, but it did. Maybe it was reading Huckleberry Finn when I was a girl and day dreaming about building a raft and going off for an adventure. Or maybe it was knowing that them cabins were something so luxurious I might never see anything like them in this lifetime.

Once she told me she'd already plunked down the money for the reservations, I was a gonner. I uncrossed my arms and nodded my head and said, yes. I'd love to go for a ride on the Mississippi Queen.

We didn't have far to go to board. The riverboat was making a stopover at Portsmouth and she had made arrangements for it to let us on.

I think Lula Faye was trying to be kind to me, or maybe she was just being selfish and dragging me along for the company. I don't know. It don't matter anyhow. The fact was that here

I had the opportunity to float down the river on that beautiful paddle wheeler and I could hardly stand myself I was so excited.

There was a problem, though. I'm no clothes horse and I didn't have nothing in my closet fit to wear for something like that. I really didn't.

People in South Shore are used to me. They are so used to seeing me around town they'd be shocked if I ever walked down the street in anything except one of my house dresses, ankle socks and tennis shoes. As long as I was clean and modest, I didn't much care what people thought. In most cases, I already knew enough about them and their families to not be particularly impressed with anything they might or might not think about me. When you're talking to someone and can remember the day in first grade when they suddenly had a puddle around their desk and trying to pretend it weren't theirs, it's hard not to feel pretty at ease around them even if they are driving a shiny new truck or are running for county sheriff.

Problem was, I didn't know anybody that was going to be on that fancy paddle wheeler except Lula Faye. I figured they'd all take one look at me and think I didn't know how to dress myself. Which weren't exactly true, but when you're living on nothing but Social Security a body sometimes has to choose between dressing good and eating good. I usually chose to eat, which meant I needed to go shopping in the worst way before we took off.

"Oh, don't worry," Lula Faye scoffed. "Just bring your undies and toothbrush and we'll buy you some nice clothes after we get on the boat."

I hated to tell her, but my undies weren't nothing to brag about, either.

So, before I hardly knew what was happening, Lula Faye had one of her neighbors drive us over to Portsmouth, and the next thing I knew, we were standing there waiting for the boat to dock. I had a lot of thoughts racing through my head while I waited. Like what on earth was I doing, me a seventy-two year old woman, gallivanting off on some wild adventure with my cousin who was nearly as old as me and both of us probably needing to have better sense.

And then, suddenly, while I was debating about maybe just changing my mind and walking back across the bridge—I heard the sound of a giant calliope a'dancing on the wind, and then the Mississippi Queen paddle boat came around the river bend. I felt like I was suddenly about ten years old and could hardly get my breath for wanting to be on that big, beautiful, thing so bad.

Lula Faye must have felt me stiffen beside her with anticipation. I saw her look at me with this smirk of satisfaction on her face.

"You glad I invited you now?" she asked.

I had to swallow before I could speak. "It's a pretty boat."

"Yes," she said. "Now promise me you'll relax and enjoy yourself."

Well I knew I could promise to enjoy myself, but relax? I didn't think that was going to happen.

We were the only passengers getting on at Portsmouth and Lula Faye had to make arrangements to have that happen. Most boardings took place in Memphis or Cincinnati or some other big town. Portsmouth was hardly a dot on the map, but enough money can get a person nearly anything—and even though it had only been a month, Lula Faye had already figured that out.

You'd a thought we were royalty, the way the crew made over us as they led us on board. Me in my church dress and tennis shoes thanking people for every little thing, and Lula Faye acting like she had been born to being treated like she was something special. It occurred to me that if Lula Faye asked for the crusts to be cut off her sandwiches for the rest of her life, it was probably going to happen.

It was nine o'clock in the morning when the boat got there, and it was already a hot day in July. I felt like I was living a dream as I walked up the plank.

I told you that boat looked like a fancy decorated wedding cake, and it did. Every level had a big porch with rocking chairs. One of the staff, a nice boy with a thick accent from Memphis, led us to our cabins. We passed by lots of people enjoying theirselves by a'rocking and looking out at the river. I felt like I needed to pinch myself to see if it was all real.

The room he led me to was about the same size as my bedroom at home—which is to say tiny. But it was beautiful and elegant. Even had a flat-screen TV. Prettiest room I'd ever seen. The bed looked so fluffy I had to sit down on it the minute the crew boy left and closed the door.

Lula came hurrying on back to my room after the boy had left her at hers.

"So," Lula Faye said. "What do you think?"

All I could do was sit there all goggle-eyed. "I think I need to get me a job on this here boat because I don't never want to leave!"

She laughed and sat down beside me. "Remember when we used to talk about what it would be like to be one of them rich people who could afford to take trips on these things?"

"I surely do."

"Well," she fell back against the bed, tossing her feet in the air and giggling. "I guess some dreams come true, 'cause here we are!"

Lula Faye was a giggler when we were young but I hadn't heard that giggle for a long time and I realized I'd missed it. That's what this moment felt like to me right now, like the years had fallen away from me and my cousin and we were telling secrets to each other back in our granny's upstairs bedroom. Except whoever put this room together was a lot better decorator than our granny ever was. Later on, after I'd had supper and took my shower, said my prayers, and crawled beneath them sheets—well, Granny's rough-dried sheets felt like sandpaper compared to them on the Mississippi Queen. There's a reason them river cruises cost so much.

First thing we did after I'd put my few things in one of the drawers and shoved my satchel out of sight in the back of the little closet, was we went exploring on the boat. At first it bothered me a little trying to walk on deck with the shore line scooting along beside me. Made me feel a little caty-wampus in my head and I kept listing over to one side until I got used to it. Everyone acted nice to us although I had a sneaking suspicion they thought I'd just escaped for a break from the kitchen. People were dressed up a little bit more than even I had expected. I guess when you spend thousands of dollars to sail down the river it stands to reason you'd dress up to honor that fact.

Eventually we ran across a small dress shop and Lula Faye was determined I try on some new clothes. Nobody else was in the shop, so me and Lula Faye had a big time playing dress up. I made the mistake of asking the sales clerk how much everything cost, and about had a heart-attack when she told me.

"I'll just put everything back real careful like," I said.

"No." Lula Faye whipped out a shiny new black platinum credit card. "This is on me." Then she started instructing the sales clerk to gather up this and that for herself and a whole lot of other things she thought I needed.

"I can't let you do that." I grabbed her arm. I meant what I said. No way was I going to let Lula Faye pay for my clothes too. Her paying for the boat ride was bad enough.

Lula Faye shook my hand off. "I can't spend what I got if I spend like crazy for the rest of my life," she said. "This will make me happy."

Then she handed the card to the sales clerk. "Don't take a penny from her for anything," Lula Faye said. "I mean it."

I stood back and watched while that clerk folded away all them pretty things in white tissue paper and fancy boxes. That's not something they do at the Dollar Store.

A young crew member took our purchases to our rooms while me and Lula Faye argued.

"I weren't raised taking no handouts," I told Lula Faye. "I ain't wearing these. I'm taking them back soon as you're not around."

"You ever read them Victorian novels where an old woman hires a companion to travel with her?" Lula Faye said. I guess I need to tell you that she was always reading novels when she was young.

"I guess," I said, although I never did.

"Think of it like that. I didn't want to take the trip alone and I hired you to go with me," she said.

"Hornswaggled me into it is more like it," I said.

"Consider yourself my employee if it makes you feel any better, and the clothes as part of the deal," Lula Faye said. "Seriously. This wasn't your idea to come along. I did hornswaggle you. I also needed to get out of town for a while and I didn't want to go alone. Like I said before. Relax and enjoy it."

And so I did. I might be old, and I might be honest, and I might be determined to pay my own way. But I ain't stupid.

Our trip was going to take us all the way to New Orleans and then back up the Ohio River. Lula Faye had gotten one of the longer cruises they offered. So there we went, floating down that big ole' Ohio River with calliope music playing at every town, a big paddle wheel turning, and us a'hanging over the rail, waving to the people on the river bank.

If people could have seen inside of us, they would have seen two little girl cousins dreaming dreams and feeling the river wind in our hair. No doubt we just looked like two old fools too excited to act like we had good sense and you know what? I didn't care. Not too many people get to live their dream, but I was living mine. At least for the next few days.

"Now aren't you happy you came?" Lula Faye said. "I told you we'd have fun."

Well actually, she hadn't said that we'd have fun. What she said was she needed to get out of town but I was too happy to care.

It don't pay to let yourself get too happy, my mama always said. She said if you get too happy it draws the attention of the devil and it's best for a body never to do that. The devil is a wily creature that don't want nobody to be happy and will find underhanded ways to make you miserable that you don't see coming. My mama was almost always right.

"Well, hello there!" A man in a fancy suit was walking along the deck and tipped his hat. Men don't wear hats all that much anymore unless it's a baseball cap, but he was wearing a formal black one. He saw us waving at the river bank and giggling together so he stopped and leaned against the railing beside us. "You ladies seem to be having a jolly good time."

It seemed odd to hear the words "jolly good" coming from a grown man's mouth, but he had a British accent so I figured it was okay. Not something I was used to hearing in South Shore, Kentucky though.

"Oh, we are!" Lula Faye said gaily. "We are just having the best time!"

I glanced over at where he was standing on the other side of Lula Faye. She was looking out at the shore line like she wasn't paying no attention to him. The Ohio is a pretty river and has nice scenery. He didn't seem to notice me watching him. The expression on his face wasn't like a man just being friendly, it was like he was evaluating her.

It made me shiver for an instant but I didn't want to let anything rain on our little parade, so I brushed it off. I told myself he was just one nicely dressed, well-spoken middle-aged man passing the day. Nothing to be afraid of. After a bit, he wished us a "good day" and wandered off.

You'd think by the time a woman hits seventy-two she'd know enough to pay attention when someone gives her the shivers, but not Yours Truly. Nope. Our preacher's always telling us to think the best of everybody and I try to. That kind of thinking might work for being around God-fearing people from South Shore who might be sitting beside you in a pew, but it don't always work out in the real world. I shoulda seen right then and there that the man with a fancy-sounding accent was a wolf in sheep's clothing.

But I told myself I was just being silly, and went back to enjoying the scenery myself.

Lula Faye turned and kinda looked after him a mite longer than she should have as he walked away.

"That was a nice man," she said.

"Uh huh." I was certain I saw a snapping turtle floating along on top of the water.

"Good-looking, too." Lula Faye said.

"Uh huh." I wondered what it would feel like to have a big house like the one I was watching pass by with a pretty yard that went all the way down to a river dock.

That was a mistake. I shoulda been paying more attention. I shoulda gone to the ship's captain that very instant and told him to pull over and let me drag Lula Faye off the boat. But I didn't. I was concentrating way too hard on having a good time. I'd also allowed myself to forget who Lula Faye's mama was. All them years of Lula Faye's being a good Baptist had lulled me into a false sense of security. Her playing the lottery could have warned me that her Baptist training was starting to wear a little thin. Sometimes apples really don't fall far from the tree.

Supper (although they called it 'dinner' on the boat like city people do) was a dress-up affair. We both went to our room and primped beforehand. That's what the new dresses were for, Lula Faye had informed me.

It's been a long, long time since I thought I was worth anyone's time to bother to look at. I got a tolerable good mind and more determination than is probably good for me at my age, but I don't get many second glances. If I do I usually check to see if my slip is dragging on the ground or if I'm trailing toilet paper from my shoes.

I kind of enjoyed getting ready for dinner. I slipped on my favorite of the pretty dresses, and brushed my hair back. The new girl down at the beauty shop had cut it shorter than usual and I was beginning to warm up to the length of it. Then I put on my new sparkly ear bobs and necklace and slipped my feet into new shiny black low-heeled shoes, and then I turned around, took a good long look at myself in the full-length mirror and just about lost my teeth.

I've never run to fat like some of my daddy's people. I inherited some height from him, too, and I've always done hard work so my skin don't sag as much as some old ladies. The silver-black dress Lula Faye had bought me hung just right. My hair, wearing that dress, looked more silver than gray.

Like I said before, sometimes it seems like a person turns old overnight. One day you're six years old playing marbles in the dirt, and the next thing you know you're sixty and having a hard time getting up out of a low chair. I'd never been a good-looking girl. I weren't cute and cuddly as a kid, and I was awkward and gangly as a young woman. I was tall and what my mama called "raw boned."

I don't have any big mirrors at home. Just Mama's bureau mirror that shows what you look like from the waist up, and then there's the mirror over the sink in the bathroom. I've never been one for looking into mirrors in the first place. What I hadn't never noticed before was that the rawboned awkwardness of my younger days had gone away, and what I saw in that full-length mirror was a tall woman with short silver hair wearing a dress that made her look strong and dignified.

I was not beautiful by any means, not even close, but I looked like a woman who'd faced life head on and done the best she could with what she was given. My hands weren't exactly dainty, but they were capable hands. They could grow their own food, or put together a nice quilt, or wring a chicken's neck and pluck it if need be to keep from going hungry. As I stared at the woman in the mirror I realized that I looked like a person I'd want to know...and that was a revelation.

Not everyone in this world likes themselves. Seems that there are a lot of people who spend most of their lives being about half-mad at everyone else for who and what they've let themselves become, or trying to pretend to be something they're not. But none of that had ever been a problem to me. I was who I was and somehow with the help of a nice dress, that feeling somehow translated itself into the dignified woman I saw in that mirror.

"Well don't you look nice!" Lula Faye's eyes lit up when she came to my door and saw me. "I guess I won't scare nobody."

"Not in that dress, you won't," Lula Faye said. "We're stopping for a few hours at Cincinnati tomorrow. Maybe we'll get to do some more shopping. I think I'm getting the knack of spending money now that I don't have the whole town watching over my shoulder."

I have to admit, as much as it shames me now, the prospect of spending more of Lula Faye's money was starting to appeal to me, too.

"Just promise me you won't go finding any more dead bodies this trip," Lula Faye said.

She laughed at her little joke and so did I. It didn't seem like nothing bad could ever happen on this lovely boat.

And that was my next mistake. Getting lulled into thinking we were safe just because everything was so nice and grand and beautiful. The Bible says that the Devil is always out there roaming around like a hungry lion looking for someone to eat up and I'm here to tell you that that's the God's honest truth.

We walked into the dining room for dinner and as I looked over the sea of white hair, I noted that most of our fellow travelers were about the age to have been on the Lawrence Welk show back when it was still being broadcast live. That made sense I suppose. Not too many young people, especially them with kids, can afford to ride on the Mississippi Queen. Some of the women were wearing jewelry that probably cost a whole lot more than my house.

So I was surprised when Lula Faye and I were escorted to the Captain's table. I mean, we were just nobodies from South Shore. It turned out that the fancy-suited man had recognized Lula Faye from a picture he'd seen in a newspaper and he'd informed the captain that the ship had a celebrity in its midst. We didn't know about all that at the time, of course. That came later.

As we approached the table, I glanced at the captain who was standing at the head of it and I immediately began digging around in my mind trying to figure out why he looked so familiar.

Then he introduced himself and I knew exactly why he looked familiar. For a minute the coincidence of who he was took my breath away and I could barely speak.

He had aged well. Very well. He had a military bearing and a comfort about meeting people that had been missing when he was nineteen, which was the last time I'd seen him. Here I was, on the Mississippi Queen, being introduced to the only boy who'd ever kissed me or even acted like he wanted to.

Most people probably have a love story of some kind tucked away in their hearts. Even if that love story was only a private crush on someone and nobody ever knew about it. Captain Evan Wilson was my one and only love story. It weren't much of a one but it was the only one I ever had.

I thought I had put that story away a long time ago but it turned out to my surprise that it made me a little dizzy meeting up with him like this. It felt like I imagined it would feel if a person came up from the depths of the ocean too quickly and got the bends. I felt a little sick to the stomach, a little woozy in the head, and definitely weak in the knees. Of course the uniform he was wearing didn't exactly hurt my eyes.

I'm just an old fool. That's what I am.

I counseled at a local church camp one summer when I was nineteen and there was this walk under the stars to my cabin with a tall young man I'd come to admire. Suddenly there was this quick, surprising, good-night kiss. Unfortunately, that kiss came too late in the summer to follow up on. It was the night before the campers and counselors scattered back to their homes the next morning.

He was from Lexington, which seemed like a world away back then when most kids didn't have cars and long-distance telephone calls were expensive and saved for emergencies only. But writing letters was still an option. Not an option I felt I could initiate, though. Girls didn't do things like that back then. At least good girls didn't. In the confusion of getting the campers sorted out and parents trying to talk to me about their kids, the morning passed way too quickly.

I guess someone came to give Evan a ride home and I never saw him ever again.

I heard a rumor through a friend of a friend that he joined the Navy a month after camp let out. I never heard another word about him, or from him.

It was soon after that I got my job at Selby Shoe Company and I put any thoughts about Evan Wilson behind me. I eventually heard he'd made a career out of the Navy. That was all I knew. Daddy got sick and I needed to help Mama take care of him. That one evening walk to my cabin during summer camp was my one little flutter of excitement over a boy. It weren't much but I never forgot it.

Introductions were made all around the table. I have to admit, I didn't pay much attention to what was being said. I was too busy giving myself a talking to. Doreen, I was saying. Try to act like you got good sense. There's no way on earth that important man is going to remember you.

"Doreen Sizemore," I said, and shook hands with him. I was determined not to act like I'd ever known him. He'd probably kissed a lot of women over the years. I was certain he'd forgotten that one little itty bitty kiss and the awkward girl he gave it to such a long, long time ago.

There's some men who get better looking with age and Evan Wilson was one of 'em. I couldn't help but notice the fact that there was no wedding ring on his finger.

"Doreen Sizemore?" He kinda cocked his head to one side and focused in on me. "I used to know a Doreen Sizemore. It was at summer camp in Kentucky when I was nineteen. Right before I joined the Navy. We were both counselors."

I've had a long life and I've seen a lot of things. There's

not much that embarrasses or bothers me anymore. At least I thought it didn't. But my old heart betrayed me. I felt myself flushing until it felt like I was as red in the face as the red roses they had sitting in a vase in the middle of the table.

Lula Faye was busy talking with the man in the fancy suit with the British accent but I didn't pay a whole lot of attention to that. I was too busy trying to stop myself from blushing like a school girl. I wished the captain would look at someone else while I got my composure back. But he didn't and I didn't.

"Yes, I was at summer camp," I croaked.

"I thought that was you," he said. "You still have that swimmer's build and I'd remember them dark eyes anywhere."

Swimmer's build? I had a swimmer's build? I never knew that. He remembered my eyes?

If there had been a couch handy I'd of probably swooned onto it.

"I remember how you used to dive headfirst into the water from the float they had out in the middle of the lake. You were so graceful and such a strong swimmer. I enjoyed watching you."

"I—I liked the water," I stuttered.

"If I remember right, it took me all summer to get up enough nerve to kiss you. I kicked myself for months for being so timid that I waited until the very end."

Everyone else had been busy greeting each other and saying polite things to each other, but I noticed that the conversation had suddenly ground to a stop and everyone was looking at the two of us with a whole lot more interest than I was comfortable with. That included Lula Faye, who had a big grin on her face. She was enjoying the situation way too much.

I couldn't be upset with her, though. I was too grateful. It was very nice to meet up with Evan Wilson again. It was even nicer to meet up with him looking better than I'd looked in years. I silently thanked her from the bottom of my heart for buying the pretty clothes I was wearing.

I think I ate something that evening but I don't remember what. All I remember is pushing things around on my plate. I tend to lose my appetite when I'm nervous.

All of us made small talk. There was a piano player in the background playing some kind of jazz. It was all so unreal. The beautiful boat. Everybody all dressed up. Knowing I'd once kissed the captain of the ship! I didn't know what to talk about. My life had been Selby Shoes and taking care of Mama and Daddy and my baby brother and sister and going to church. It had been an honest life, but it felt small and insignificant sitting here with all these other people. I couldn't think of a thing to say.

Lula Faye later told me she thought she'd help me out since the cat had evidently got my tongue.

"My cousin, Doreen here," she said. "Is a bona fide sleuth."

"Really?" Evan looked interested and so did all the others. "I want to hear more about this."

"She goes around solving murders." Lula Faye said. "The police consult with her on cases."

Actually, from what I'd seen, the police were usually flat out annoyed that I was involved at all, but my mama had taught me never to correct people in front of others unless it was life or death, so I let Lula Faye's statement stand as though it were a fact. Truth be told, down deep I was grateful to my cousin for making me out to be a whole lot more interesting than I was.

"Only three," I said, modestly.

"Only three what?" Evan prompted.

"Um, murders."

That started a conversation around the table about the fact that no one else had ever stumbled upon even one murder, let alone three.

The fancy-talking man—he said his name was Nolan Withersham—said he'd once had a corpse discovered at the perimeter of his estate, but that he'd been in the south of France at the time. His groundskeeper had contacted the proper authorities who'd eventually informed him that it had been a local man out taking a walk who had died of a coronary. He said that nothing as exotic as murder had ever happened near him.

I saw Lula Faye's eyes brighten listening to him talk about his estate in England and his groundskeeper and I could just about read her mind. It was probably them little sandwiches that her mama used to make for company that did it. My cousin was used to finer things. I'm afraid that living on a country estate in England with a well-dressed man like Nolan Whithersham probably sounded like the kind of life Lula Faye could get used to real quick. One thing for sure, Lula Faye wouldn't have no problem with bossing servants around.

When dinner was over and Nolan offered to accompany Lula Faye back to her room, she didn't say no. I couldn't fault her none. When Captain Wilson offered to take me around for a personal tour of the ship, I weren't about to say no either. Not in this lifetime.

The private tour took some time. It was a big ship and Evan was pretty enthusiastic about it. Frankly, he reminded me of a small boy showing a friend his favorite toy, but I could tell he was no little boy in the eyes of his staff. It was obvious that they respected and liked him.

He showed me everything from the paddle wheel and the steam pipes to where laundry was done. By the time Evan got around to showing me the pilot's house on the top, it was pretty late. I didn't even know we had made it to the pilot house until he was sitting me down at a little table and a waiter—I think they call them something else on the ship but

I forget what—had brought us a late-night treat of cheese cake and ice cream and a few other pretty little things all arranged on a fancy plate.

I nibbled at them sweets while I enjoyed listening to Evan talk about his career in the Navy and how he ended up being the captain of this beautiful ship. The whole time I kept thinking about here I was, sitting up high, watching a pilot quietly vigilant as he steered that big ship down the Ohio River while the captain paid attention to me. It was the most romantic thing I'd ever lived through. It felt like I was inside a movie.

Then Evan looked deep into my eyes and said, "Now, Doreen. Enough about me. Tell me all about what you've been doing since we saw each other last."

I didn't have nothing to say.

"Do you have grandchildren?" he prompted. "A career you loved? Is there a husband back home? What kind of a life did that lovely and courageous girl I once knew have?"

Lovely and courageous. I knew I was going to disappoint this man, but it's not in my nature to make things up except maybe for the stories I used to tell my brother when he was little.

"I never amounted to nothing special," I admitted. "I got a job working at a shoe factory. Daddy got sick soon after that summer at camp, and I helped Mama take care of him for a long time. Then Mama got sick and I took care of her. By the time they had passed on, there weren't nobody much of a marrying age left in South Shore that I liked the looks of so I never got married or had any children. They shut down the Selby factory a few years back and I did grocery clerking for a while. I got me a little house down by the river—it ain't much but it's all I need--and I got me a pretty good church to go to."

"What about being a sleuth?"

"Oh, that weren't nothing but me being at the wrong place

at the wrong time and using a little bit of common sense to figure things out. I ain't no real sleuth. Don't want to be one, neither."

It sounded so small after hearing all about his exciting travels and career. But if there's one thing I've learned it's that it's best to just be honest up front about things. Saves a person a whole lot of worry and grief later.

"You had a little brother?" Evan said. "Whatever happened to him?"

"He moved to Texas. I was down there for a long spell last year helping his wife get through the chemo. She's doing real good now but I don't care all that much for how my brother turned out. Mama and me kind of spoiled him when he was little. He ain't never gotten over it."

"And your sister?"

"She passed on about ten years ago," I said.

I'd laid my everyday life out there in front of him. It weren't nothing special and I knew it. I was also starting to feel the weight of how late it was. My new shoes had begun to hurt a long time ago, and the girdle Lula Faye had insisted I buy was beginning to cut into my waist something awful.

"Sounds to me like you spent your whole life taking care of your family," Evan said.

"Yep. Guess so." That girdle was starting to get on my nerves. I wanted to get back to my cabin and yank it off. "That pretty much sums it up. I wouldn't be here now if it weren't for Lula Faye winning the lottery and making me come with her. She even bought this dress I'm a'wearing."

Then about the time I started figuring that I'd probably bored the man to tears, Evan reached across the table and laid his hand over mine. "I'm so glad Lula Faye brought you on this trip," he said. "I'm looking forward to getting to know you better."

"There ain't that much more to get to know," I said, surprised.

"Selfless women are rare these days," Evan said. "Honest ones even rarer. I've enjoyed tonight more than you can possibly know.

Just then the pilot had to interrupt us about some river traffic ahead and it needed the captain's attention.

"I have to deal with this and it could take a while, so I'm going to have someone walk you back to your room. I'd like to spend more time with you during this cruise if you're willing."

My annoyance over the girdle evaporated after that little speech. My feet felt just fine and dandy, too. I'd never realized before that the attention of a handsome man could be an effective pain-killer but there it is. That spot of arthritis I got in my left knee seemed to have left me as well when he took my hand and led me to the door. Some young deck hand was already waiting to walk me back to my room. I don't know how Evan managed to get him there so fast.

When I woke up the next morning, I found out that we were docked outside of Cincinnati. That was no surprise. I'd seen that on the itinerary we'd been given. I also knew that there was going to be some free time to do some wandering around, sight-seeing, riding in the tour bus, or shopping time. I surely hoped Lula Faye would be as good as her word and we could do some more shopping. It had been a long time since I'd cared about being anything except clean and modest, but that had changed the minute Evan Wilson laid his hand over mine.

Let me tell you something. This was one seventy-two-year-old lady who all of a sudden wanted to look good!

The next several days were like living in a dream. Them two fancy rooms of Lula Faye and mine, and good food I didn't have to cook, available several times a day. Evan was a busy man with a huge boat to drive and all, but we ran into each other from time to time and he kind of lit up whenever he saw me. We would talk for a few minutes before he would rush on. He'd ask if I were enjoying myself and if there was anything I needed. Usually we'd be interrupted before we'd got two words out because so many people wanted his attention. Every time I ate in the main dining area I was automatically seated at the captain's table whether he was there or not which made some of the other women act a little miffed.

I kept wishing I knew for sure whether or not there was still a Mrs. Wilson back home, but he never mentioned a wife. It was a worry to me. Not that I expected to marry the man. Gracious! The time had passed long ago for that kind of foolishness, but still, it made me feel good that he seemed to like talking to me. And I mean "to" me. Even though he was the captain and all, he never talked down at me.

I didn't see as much of Lula Faye as I had expected, and that was fine. She seemed to be awfully interested in that Nolen Withersham. He told her that he was recently widowed and taking this cruise to help mend his broken heart. It worried me when Lula Faye started taking on sort of an English accent like she was already practicing to be Lady of the Manor.

With Lula Faye spending every spare minute with Nathan, I had to walk the decks and amuse myself by myself a good bit, but that weren't hard. There were a lot of things to do and people to talk to. I'm usually not the most social person in the world but the thing about a cruise is that you know it is going to end at some time and everyone will go home. It ain't like when you strike up a conversation with someone you don't know back home and then wonder if you're going to have to be friends with them for the rest of your life whether you like them or not.

A couple days later, I got ready for breakfast and went to

get Lula Faye. Even if we weren't together all that much during the rest of the day we tried to at least have breakfast together and get caught up. Nolan Withersham weren't an early riser, so we usually had breakfast all to ourselves.

Lula Faye was not up yet when I knocked on her door. She came to open up and was as disheveled and sleepy-eyed as I'd ever seen anybody.

"What happened to you?" I asked.

"N-nothing," she said, glancing in the mirror as she tried to smooth her hair down.

She sounded kinda guilty, but I figured she was just ashamed of sleeping in so late. Lula Faye and me do come from people who know how to get up early and get a day's work done. Of course, we were on vacation so I didn't know why she would feel guilty about sleeping late. It weren't like she had anything she actually had to do. Considering the fact that she'd won the lottery, I figured she'd never have to do anything ever again if she didn't want to.

"Come in and order some breakfast to be brought here to the room," Lula Faye said. "I don't want to go to the dining room. You can eat while I shower."

I'd never ordered anything remotely resembling room service in my life, but there was a little menu card beside the phone, and I found out that it was easier than I thought telling someone what to bring me. I already knew what Lula Faye wanted. The woman eats oatmeal for breakfast every morning of her life. Her mama told her once that it was good for a woman's complexion and Lula Faye never forgot that. It mighta worked for her mama, but from what I could see Lula Faye's complexion weren't any better than any other woman's her age.

Then I crawled up onto Lula Faye's bed and used a remote to turn on the television set while I waited for someone to bring us a ready-cooked breakfast. I had to admit, rich people could have a real easy life if they wanted to. I reminded myself not to get used to it, though. I had a regular life to get back to after this fairy tale was over.

But my normal life seemed awfully far away right then. There's something about being on a river cruise that makes a person feel like time is standing still. With no responsibilities to worry about except to relax and enjoy myself, I felt like I was sort of drifting through each day and it felt real good. Some days we stopped at little towns and shopped and walked and did some sight-seeing. At night after supper, I would tuck myself into that snug little room with the expensive sheets and good bed that didn't sag in the middle. There was something to look forward to every day of this cruise and I was determined to savor every second of it.

At least I thought there was a lot to look forward to until Lula Faye got herself accused of murder.

I knew I shouldn't have let her talk me into going on that cruise. Baptists playing the lottery just ain't natural. I shoulda known something bad was bound to happen and it surely did.

I thought Lula Faye seemed a little "off" at breakfast a couple days before the cruise was going to be over. Kinda clingy. Didn't say much, though. She kept looking around worried-like, no matter what we were doing. If I pointed out something interesting on the river bank, I could tell she weren't really paying attention. After breakfast, we were going to be given the option to go on shore and Lula Faye said she weren't interested.

"What's wrong with you," I asked. "Even I'm enjoying myself and I hate to travel."

Lula Faye sort of bit her lip and traced her finger on the white linen table cloth they had on the breakfast table. "I might have made a big mistake," she said.

This was the first time I'd ever heard Lula Faye ever say

anything about her having made a mistake. Even when we were little bitty girls she always acted like she was right about everything even when she was dead wrong. This new behavior scared me and when I'm scared I get irritable.

"A mistake? What did you do, Lula Faye?" I said. "Spit it out!"

"I might have given some money away," she said.

"Might?"

"Okay," she admitted. "I did give some money away but I didn't mean to. I thought I was just lending it to someone."

"How much?" I knew it couldn't have been too bad. Lula Faye, with the one exception of taking me on this cruise and buying me some clothes, was one of the most tight-fisted people I knew unless there were people watching. Then she'd give a few dollars to charity or put a couple quarters in the collection plate.

"A few thousand." Her eyes wandered away.

"How few a thousand?"

"Maybe a hundred."

"A hundred thousand?"

She nodded, her eyes downcast.

"Dollars?"

She kept looking down at the table. Embarrassed.

"Who on earth did you give a hundred thousand dollars to?"

"Mr. Withersham."

"The Englishman?"

She nodded again.

"Why?" I suddenly found myself tapping my foot to beat the band. It was a habit I only had when I got upset, so I made myself stop. It weren't my money she'd given away, but I couldn't understand what had gotten into my cousin to make her do something that strange. She'd only known the man four days.

"He said he needed a small loan for a short time. He said his estate manager, who takes care of his finances, was ill and he was unable to get his funds wired to the United States right now."

"I can understand loaning him a few dollars," I said. "Maybe even a few hundred dollars. But a hundred thousand? What did you think he was going to do with it? Buy the whole ship?"

Lula Faye couldn't seem to hold her head up one second longer. She laid it down on the table even though it looked funny and people stared.

"Is your friend okay, ma'am?" One elderly gentleman at the next table leaned over and asked me. "Does she need a physician?"

"What I think she needs," I said, "is to have her head examined."

"Oh. Psychiatric problems?" he asked.

"Definitely," I answered.

I leaned over and whispered into Lula Faye's ear. "What did Mr. Fancy Pants need the money for?"

Lula Faye mumbled something into the crook of her arm and I had to ask her to repeat it. When she did, my jaw dropped so fast I almost unhinged something. I had to ask her to repeat it again.

"You heard me right," she said. "I loaned him the money so that he could buy me a really nice engagement ring once we got to New Orleans."

"An engagement ring?"

She nodded.

"You thought you were getting engaged?"

She nodded, this time sniffling.

"When did you even have a chance to get your hands on

that much money?" I asked. "It's not like there's a bank on board."

"When we went ashore yesterday."

"And you didn't tell me?"

"Nolan said I shouldn't say anything because it would be hard on you to find out that I would be marrying and moving to England and living a luxurious life while you were still stuck in Kentucky. He said we should break it to you slowly. Let you get used to the fact that we were a couple."

"Nolan said all that, did he?" I was so angry I could have smacked him. "So where is he?"

"That's just it," Lula Faye said. "I don't know. We were supposed to go wedding ring shopping together when we got to New Orleans. He said there was a jeweler there that would make me something unique and beautiful. We were going to be married here on the ship at the end of the cruise and fly out to England the next day."

"And when was the last time you saw him?"

"Yesterday," she said. "Right after I gave him the money for the ring."

It weren't him taking the money that was making me so mad. A hundred thousand dollars is a drop in the bucket considering how much Lula Faye had won. I admit that Lula Faye sometimes gets so bossy I don't like her all that much, but no one had the right to break my cousin's heart. Especially not a fancy-talking foreigner.

I'd read once about how the lottery had destroyed a lot of people's lives who'd won. There are some folks who just can't deal with massive amounts of riches dumped on them all of a sudden. It messes with their brain and their relationships with other people. Even I felt a little ashamed. I'd let Lula Faye talk me into going on the luxury cruise that two old river rats like us had no business being on. It was obvious we were in over our heads. If me and Lula Faye wanted to take a trip on the river it would have made a whole lot more sense for us to find us an old row boat and pack us a picnic lunch. That would fit who we were a whole lot better. Instead, here we were in this mess.

"Well," I said. "I guess you've learned your lesson. Maybe it was a cheap one if it keeps you from giving away your money to every man who acts like he's in love with you."

"You really think he just up and left? That he didn't care about me at all?"

"I don't know what he cared about," I said. "All I know is his accent sounded a mite fishy to me."

Lula Faye's shoulders slumped. "You're right. I never thought I'd admit it, but I've turned into one of them sad old women who get taken in by some man pretending to be in love with me."

My mind immediately flew to Evan. He knew I didn't hardly have two dimes to rub together and never would. There was no need for him to act like he enjoyed being in my company if he didn't.

It occurred to me that not having much was a blessing I'd never realized before. At least I knew that the friends I got are really my friends. No one has any need to pay attention to me thinking they're gonna get something from me. Even my little house weren't worth much. Property values in South Shore ain't real high.

"I think what we need to do is put this whole thing behind us and try to enjoy what's left of this cruise," I said.

It was good advice, but Lula Faye was never one to listen to someone else's advice.

"No," she said. "I want to find him. I don't appreciate him lying to me like that. I thought we were in love. I thought I was going to move to England and live in a mansion and have tea in the afternoon. I thought Nolan Withersham was my soul mate."

"You only knew him for a few days!" It sounded to me like my cousin had been watching a little too much Downton Abbey on the television set. I wondered if that Nolan Withersham might have realized that an expensive cruise would be a good place to pick up rich women and fill their heads with pretty pictures about what life with him would be like.

"I know what I felt." Lula Faye said. "Don't make fun of me."

"I'm not making fun of you," I said. "I'm just saying you only knew him a few days."

"No one makes a fool out of me!" Lula Faye said. "I'm going to find him—one way or another."

Having made up her mind to go after him for revenge, Lula Faye took off to see the captain about getting Nolan found. Lula Faye on a mission was usually like watching a pro football player running down the middle of the football field knocking down everyone in his way. I decided I did not want to be around when she talked to the captain.

I finished my omelet because it was tasty, but the whole time I ate I was imagining Lula Faye getting up in Evan's face. I wished I'd never come on this trip with her.

This would be the last journey I ever took with Lula Faye and if I had my way—the last trip I took ever.

Well, after Lula Faye told Evan what Nolan had done, Evan went to Nolan's room himself. Didn't even send a crew person to do it. I guess he thought Nolan might be holed up there avoiding Lula Faye until they docked and he could get away. Of course Lula Faye had already been there a'knocking and trying to get him to come out but with no luck.

The captain, however, could get inside any room he wanted to and he did. What he found out was that Nolan weren't in his room, but everything else about Nolan was. Including his suitcases and a wallet with a driver's license in it that let them know he weren't no Nolan Withersham.

His name was Howard Shelstein and he weren't from any estate in England, he was from New Jersey. Lula Faye had been taken in by a real, honest-to-goodness scam artist.

Like I said—it just don't pay to travel.

So, now we knew who Nolan really was but we still didn't know where he was. The last time Lula Faye had seen him, they were parting ways to get ready for dinner the night before and then he just didn't show up.

It was most definitely a mystery, but since it didn't involve any dead bodies I intended to stay out of it. At least I thought I would. That was before I factored in Lula Faye's natural flair for bossiness.

There was what they called a Riverlorian who was lecturing on Mark Twain in the ship's library the next day. He was good and knew his stuff. I'm not a big reader, but I had enjoyed Twain's books when I was in school. I was enjoying getting to hear all about the Mississippi River and the steamboats that used to blow up on it on a semi-regular basis. We only had a few days left on the ship and I was trying to enjoy what was left. Then Lula Faye found me.

If Lula Faye was upset and miserable, then she expected me to be upset and miserable, too. I couldn't figure out if she just wanted revenge or if she was still of the opinion that this Nolan/Howard person was the love of her life and just needed to be found and persuaded of that fact.

Anyway, she pestered me and pestered me until I was about ready to swat her. It was like having a fly buzzing around my head.

"Has Evan found out anything yet?" she whispered while

the Riverlorian was speaking. She was acting like a child with that ADHD stuff. Couldn't sit still.

"Not that I know of," I answered.

"Will he tell you if he does?" she whispered again so loud that a couple of other people turned their heads to look at her.

"My guess is that he'd tell you if he finds out anything," I answered. "Now be quiet."

Lula Faye was just ruining the nice cruise she'd bought me. I was trying to be polite, but I'd already decided that being with an unhappy Lula Faye on an extended trip was a whole lot worse than no trip at all. I found myself almost wishing that Nolan was back here squiring her around.

The woman could buy a castle in England with the kind of money she had now if that was the kind of life she thought she needed. Why focus her entire happiness on one man who'd run away with her engagement ring money?

After she ruined the perfectly nice Riverlorian lecture, I tried getting her to focus on something else. At lunch time I convinced her to try sitting with some other people. We were supposed to mingle and get to know others. I saw a table with several other women sitting together and it had a couple of open chairs. I asked if we could join them. I was desperate for some other company besides Lula Faye.

They said I was welcome. It turned out that all of them were traveling companions from all over the country who had decided to go on this trip together. All looked to be about in their late sixties. Several were still working full-time. Ethel sold real estate and was divorced. Macie ran a clothing shop and was widowed. Jacqueline was a retired college English professor who had never married. Deborah was married to a man who owned a golf course and she said she had suggested the river cruise because she wanted to get as far away from golf as possible. All of them had been friends since college.

Lula Faye was still so upset that she wanted to tell anyone who'd listen what Nolan Withersham had done to her and how he'd disappeared. Ethel, who seemed to be a sort of no-nonsense person, excused herself to go to the bathroom and never came back. The clothing store owner tried to tell Lula Faye that she was lucky to find out what kind of a man he was before she married him, but Lula Faye didn't seem to want to hear it. The other two women didn't say much, just made a lot of sympathetic noises, but they kept glancing at each other like they'd really prefer to go find themselves another table but didn't want to be impolite and were sticking it out with us just because they were nice people.

I tried to act normal, but after a while I just sat back and watched Lula Faye monopolize the conversation. I'd seen a T-shirt once that said, "Help! I've started talking and I can't stop!" That was Lula Faye that day. She told that table everything about herself except her bra size. They were charming and kind in spite of Lula Faye's verbal flood. I wished I could hang out with them for the rest of the trip instead of Lula Faye. I was pretty sure that hearing about golf courses, clothing stores, or teaching English would be a whole lot more interesting than hearing every last detail of Nolan's brief courtship.

The next morning we finally got news, and it weren't good. Not good at all. It's hard seeing your first cousin handcuffed and drug off a boat. The police weren't nearly as careful with Lula Faye as I thought they should be. She's got a little bit of a heart condition and I thought they were handling her too rough. There was no need for handcuffs neither. Especially when someone is about to hyperventilate from fear. Lula Faye was scared and crying and I was trying to get them to ease up on her and I might have gotten a little too loud and the next thing I knew, I was sitting smack dab in a jail cell with her and wondering how on earth I'd managed to get myself in such a fix.

Turns out someone had found Nolan's body stashed away beneath a tarp on one of the emergency life boats and it was pretty obvious that he'd been murdered. Evan had called in a report of his talks with Lula Faye and she ended up being the one and only suspect—especially after they found the bloody knife that had killed him beneath Lula Faye's bedroom bureau.

She said she hadn't done it and I told her I believed her, but frankly I weren't all that sure. Remember her mama? Acting all nicey-nice and then running off with that man? And then there was Lula Faye secretly playing the lottery all them years without anyone suspecting a thing. A bloody knife beneath her bureau didn't surprise me as much as it shoulda. Truth be told, I was a little uncomfortable sharing a cell with her even if she was acting like a scared little girl and kept holding my hand like we were both six-years-old.

A ship like the Mississippi Queen with all them people aboard can't just sit around and wait on a couple of old ladies to sweat it out in a jail cell. The police went over the ship real good, found Lula Faye's fingerprints all over Nolan's room— including the shower—which I didn't want to think about. I guess she really had been convinced that Nolan was the love of her life.

So there we were. In a strange town where we didn't know nobody or have any kin, and Lula Faye arrested for murder and me as a maybe accessory to murder.

Evan did come to see us before the boat left. He was apologetic, but that didn't do us any good. He was the captain of the ship and he had to leave to keep the boat on schedule. He said he'd already have to try to make up the hours the ship had been kept so the police could do their job. People on the ship had airplane schedules to keep to get back home. He was sorry, but he had to go do his job or a whole lot of people would be missing their flights. He said he'd have our things packed up and mailed to our homes. It hurt to see him go. It hurt to have to look at him through prison bars.

That night, me and Lula Faye got a real interesting education. We shared a cell with some interesting ladies, let me tell you. There was lots of toilet water in that holding cell that night. Lots of tattoos and short skirts and pointy high heels. Made my feet hurt just to look at them.

Eventually a man with a fancy hat came and bailed all of them out. I wished someone would come and bail me out but it weren't happening.

Lula Faye had enough money for bail, of course. The problem was, murder is a serious accusation and a judge had to decide on how much bail and that hadn't happened yet. Besides, you gotta know how to find a bail bondsman and all that stuff that we'd never dealt with before.

It stood to reason that we needed a good attorney, and fast. Problem was, we were in a strange city and we didn't know any good lawyers there. Truth be told, we didn't know any good lawyers back home, neither, but we would've had people we could ask if we did.

I have some good friends. I also got a pack of relatives scattered all over the United States, but I learned something that night. If you want to evaluate the depth of your friendship with someone, just consider whether or not they would come bail you out of jail if you called and asked them to. Especially if that jail happened to be in a whole other state. I had a lot of friends, but most all of them were older women about like me. Lots of 'em had health problems. Some didn't see all that good or have the ability to drive all that far. I figured my best hope was Bobby Joe, a young cousin who lived next door to me back home. He and his wife, Esther, helped me out from time to time, but he was unemployed right now and last I'd heard his truck wasn't running all that good.

Lula Faye, for the first time in her life, had no idea what to do. None at all. The bossiness had done all gone out of her. She just kept telling me again and again that she didn't do it. That she loved Nolan/Howard and would never have hurt him even if he had stole a hundred thousand dollars from her.

I kept asking her if she had anyone who might come bail us out when the judge decided how much we would cost, but she just said she couldn't bear the humiliation of anyone back home knowing what she'd did.

In other words, we were in a pickle and as ignorant of what to do about it as two old porch dogs.

Lula Faye finally lapsed into a deep sleep, as though needing to escape the reality she was living in. While she was out, I made a decision and got permission to make my phone call. I decided not to bother Bobby Joe. He had enough to worry about.

No, I made a call that if Lula Faye had known about it, she'd have wrestled the phone out of my hand. I was glad she was passed out cold from exhaustion and fear. I'd have hated to fist-fight my cousin. Especially since I weren't entirely sure but what she'd killed that man.

The person I called was Marva, the secretary back at Lula Faye's church. Marva was one of the most quietly competent women I'd ever met. I knew if there was a way to figure out what to do in this mess, she'd be able to find it, and then keep her mouth shut about it. She might even be able to make some phone calls herself and find us a lawyer here in town that knew what he was doing.

I never dreamed the first person she'd call would be Preacher Roy. And the last thing I would have expected was for Preacher

Roy to jump in his car and drive straight to Mississippi to help us.

One thing I do know—when he came walking up to us in that jail cell, I've never been so glad to see anyone in my life. Even Lula Faye seemed relieved. Turns out that if there was one thing Preacher Roy knew outside of the scriptures it was the inside of a prison.

"What did you do, Lula Faye?" was the first thing that he said.

"I didn't do anything," she said. "And neither did Doreen. I don't know what happened on that ship, but we didn't kill anyone."

Preacher Roy nodded. Then he left. Talk about a man of few words! I don't like people who gabble all the time, but I could have used a sentence or two right then.

Some people make promises and don't deliver. Others— and they are rare—don't make promises but they make things happen. Preacher Roy was one of them kind of people. Few words, lots of action. Within the hour, a lawyer had shown up. He seemed real competent, too. Between the two of them, Preacher Roy and the lawyer, we managed to get out on bail. The lawyer left after conferring with Roy, and then Lula Faye's preacher drove us to a Holiday Inn Express and got us two rooms. One for me and Lula Faye to share and one for him. I would've been happy with a private room—I'd had just about enough of my cousin by that time, but beggars can't be choosers.

The room had two queen-sized beds in it. I showered jail off me, put my clothes back on—I didn't have any choice in clothing this time, it was the clothes on my back or nothing— and then I crawled into them sheets and kinda died for a while. I'd been through a lot and this old lady needed her rest if she was going to face another day.

It really, really don't pay to travel.

I had no idea what was going to happen to us next, except I didn't think I'd get the death penalty. I weren't so sure about Lula Faye. She might. Being so far away from home there was no telling what might happen to us in the state of Mississippi which was kinda like a foreign land to us two. All I wanted was to go back home where I belonged, crawl in bed, and pull the covers over my head until this nightmare went away. Problem was, even though we were free to walk around for now, we weren't free to leave the state.

Thank goodness for Preacher Roy. He might not be a big talker, but he was good at listening and Lula Faye needed a whole lot of listening to. I guess I did, too. We had big troubles and talking to Roy was easy. Maybe it was because with him having spent so many years in prison, we didn't feel like he was going to spend much time judging us. He just wanted to help and he did.

We got questioned by the police again. They were pretty thorough. Their biggest problem with Lula Faye was how come they had found a knife in her room. Them doors locked automatically. About the only people who could've gotten in when she wasn't looking was her and maybe some crew members—except the crew didn't exactly have open access—except the cleaning lady and she didn't have no reason to kill Nolan/Howard. Lula Faye got to crying so hard while they were questioning her that she threw up. They were a little more careful with her after that.

With me, the police weren't all that happy about the murders I'd been attached to in the past. I tried to tell them that the only time it ever happened was when I left home—and I promised them that if they'd let me go home I'd never, ever leave South Shore again. They chuckled at that, but they did question me about my relationship with Captain Wilson.

I guess someone on the ship had brought it up, as though I actually had a relationship with the captain.

Truth be told, it hurt my feelings a little that Captain Evan Wilson had just gone on ahead and left us behind like he did. Even though I knew he had to, it still hurt. I'd gotten the impression that he was sweet on me, and from what I could tell he weren't giving me and my predicament much thought right now. I realized that Lula Faye weren't the only one who'd gone stupid over a man on this trip.

I lost sleep them two nights we spent in that Holiday Express down in Natchez while the lawyer who Preacher Roy got for us did whatever it is that lawyers do. I'd lay there thinking over everything, wishing I could come up with a solution to the whole murder problem while Lula Faye lay there snoring away beside me.

It would have been nice if she'd of gone ahead and gotten herself her own room, but she said she was afraid to stay by herself now--but she was dead to the world whenever her head hit the pillow. How that woman could sleep under the circumstances, I have no idea, but some people deal with stress by sleeping a lot. I guess she was one of them kind of people.

I spent the biggest part of my time in Natchez trying to figure out who might have kilt that Nolan/Howard fellow. I guess I'd started to think I actually did have a bit of sleuth in me, and thought if I just tried real hard I could solve this one.

Problem is the only person I could come up with who had a good reason to kill that fake British man was my cousin who was a'snoring right there beside me. Was she capable of it? I thought maybe she was. I remember when her daddy took a notion to raise chickens to eat. He bought a box full of baby chicks and raised them up so he could butcher and freeze them.

Them baby chicks were awful cute and me and Lula Faye cuddled them and played with them and even claimed a couple of them for our own and named them. Which was fine until it came to butchering time. We were still pretty young and I couldn't stand it. I had to run home to my mama when I saw what my uncle was fixing to do. But not Lula Faye. She seemed to take it all in stride. That girl could cut a pet chicken's head off, pluck it, cut it up, watch Aunt Belle fry it, and then eat it like there was nothing to it.

Me? I learned to do what had to be done, but it never come easy. I always got real queasy when I had to eat something I'd been good friends with the day before.

The subconscious is an amazing thing. Daddy used to solve math puzzles in his head while he was sleeping at night. He'd go to bed stumped and wake up with the answer.

I wondered if this could happen to me and decided to give it a shot but when I did manage to get to sleep, I just kept having nightmares about being locked up and not being able to breathe. I think it was because of all the cheap perfume I'd smelled in that jail cell.

My prayer life got awful active about that time. I'd never been one of them people who spent a lot of time praying. I kinda saved it for special occasions, figuring the good Lord expected me to take care of what I could and He'd handle the stuff I couldn't. Well this was turning out to be one of them special occasions. I was worried sick and pretty much praying morning, noon, and night that my cousin weren't a murderer and the police would find that out.

The second day in Natchez, while she was in the bathroom, I confessed to Roy that I had a few doubts about my cousin's innocence. I told him about Aunt Belle and the butchering of the chickens and the secret lottery ticket buying down through the years and how crazy-upset Lula Faye had been over that old Nolan/Howard person not wanting to marry her.

"She coulda done it," I told him. "I hate to admit it, but

there's a wild streak in Lula Faye in spite of all the piano playing and Sunday-school teaching."

Roy didn't seem surprised. He just smiled this slow, amused grin.

"There's a wild streak in all of us, Doreen," he said. "Haven't you figured that out yet?"

"Not me," I said. "All I want is to get back to my little house."

"Lula Faye is a good woman," he said. "I've known some murderers in my time—shared a cell with some of them—and trust me, your cousin is no murderer."

Long about evening the second day, Roy got a phone call from the lawyer who had just heard from the police who had gotten big news from Captain Evan Wilson. Turns out the mystery had been solved right before the boat docked in New Orleans. Evan and his staff had figured out what had happened without any help from the police and all because of some missing cutlery.

It turned out that Lula Faye weren't the only person Nolan/Howard had lied to and cheated. In fact, Nolan/Howard had pulled his act on a whole lot of unsuspecting women over the years who thought he cared about them. Turns out he'd once even cheated one of the ladies we'd met at lunch that day earlier in the year. She was an intelligent business woman, but even intelligent business women sometimes need a love story so bad they are willing to overlook a few red flags that might crop up.

Ethel, that real estate lady we'd eaten with, was the one who done it. Ten years earlier, Nolan/Howard had swindled her out of the entire nest egg she'd hoped to retire on and it had been a considerable amount of money. She'd been so embarrassed and ashamed about it, she'd never told anybody. Not even the police. She'd just swallowed the loss, put all them thoughts away she'd had about retiring early and marrying the man of her dreams, and went back to work. That was back before he'd decided to turn British. Ten years had aged both of them, and it had taken her a couple days to realize who was walking around on the deck of the Mississippi Queen, but when she did, well, there was a lot of anger built up in that woman.

A woman scorned can be a lethal thing. It had not been Ethel's intention to murder the man. When she booked the cruise, she thought she was just taking a hard-earned vacation. Then she'd seen the man who had ruined her life being all cozy with Lula Faye. The thing that drove her over the edge was that he and Lula Faye had sat at their table the evening before and he hadn't even recognized her. Something that had impacted every waking moment for the past ten years had meant so little to him that he didn't even remember it or her. The man was a professional scam artist and there had been a lot of foolish women over the years.

As Ethel said in her testimony later, she'd been so angry at him that she had invited him to her room late that afternoon and confronted him. She said she just wanted to let him know what he had done to her. She told the police that if he had shown some remorse, she wouldn't have killed him, but he'd made the mistake of laughing at her. That laugh was an expensive one. It got him a death sentence.

Ethel was a big woman and he was a smallish man and ten years of built up anger gave her a whole lot more strength than normal. Earlier in the day she had ordered room service. The dishes from lunch were still there and they had included a steak knife. Roy told us that Ethel said she didn't remember stabbing the man, but knows she did it because there weren't nobody else in the room.

A steak knife ain't usually a person's first choice for a lethal weapon but there were a lot of knife wounds in that man.

Enough to kill him. Evidently, Ethel had a whole lot more anger built up than even she realized.

After it was over, she didn't know what to do, but she weren't a stupid woman. She did the thing that would cause the least suspicion. She sat the leftover plates and tray outside her door to be picked up, hung a sign asking not to be disturbed on the door handle, and went to dinner hoping to get a revelation over what to do about the dead body in her room and the weapon she'd used.

That's where me and Lula Faye came in. The whole time Lula Faye had been pouring out her heart to everyone at the dinner table, Ethel had been forming a plan. I remember how she'd excused herself long before the rest of us were done eating. Turns out she'd gone straight to Lula Faye's room and after wiping the fingerprints off the handle, she'd given that bloody steak knife a hard pitch underneath the door. Them rooms were small, and it had slid beneath the bureau. Being a real estate woman, she'd already noticed that the riverboat was so old, the wood had shrunk a tad here and there which had left a bigger gap than there shoulda been beneath the doors.

She had to wait around until it was dark to stuff his body into a lifeboat underneath a tarp. She'd spent the rest of the night cleaning up her room the best she could before the maid came in the next morning.

What she hadn't expected was for someone in the kitchen keeping track of cutlery. When Evan found out the man had been killed with a steak knife, he'd done some checking and found out there'd been one missing from Ethel's tray.

At first, Ethel said the knife had been there when she put it outside her door and Lula Faye must have picked it up when she walked past. But then the cops did that light shining thingy and found traces of blood all over Ethel's room. It's awful hard to get that stuff out no matter how hard you clean.

That was when Ethel broke down bawling and confessed everything. Suddenly, Lula Faye and me were off the hook. I was awful ashamed that I had secretly suspected my cousin of murder.

I also realized that in a way poor old Ethel had done Lula Faye a big favor. As crazy as my cousin had been about that man, no telling how long it woulda been before she realized he'd managed to pocket her fifty-two million dollars and there weren't no manor in England after all.

Preacher Roy gathered us up and we hightailed it out of there just as soon as the police were sure that Lula Faye didn't do it. Roy didn't say a lot, but that was okay. We'd heard a lot of words this week. I was ready to be real quiet for a while and I was. That's one of the nicer things about living alone—most of the time you don't have to talk to nobody unless you really want to.

Me and Lula Faye didn't see each other or call back and forth for a long time. I figured we were just plumb sick of each other.

At least that's what I thought. Later I learned that something very different was going on at Lula Faye's end to make her so quiet. She and Preacher Roy got married a few weeks later. She called to tell me, as excited as a school girl.

I had my suspicions about Preacher Roy then. I figured he was after Lula Faye's money, too. I figured he'd quit preaching altogether and just live off of her.

Once again, I was dead wrong. That marriage between Preacher Roy and Lula Faye is a match made in heaven. He can't be railroaded by her and she needs someone steady. For reasons I don't understand at all, he seems to think Lula Faye is cute as a button, and from what I can tell, he truly loves the woman. She adores him and ain't been the same person since they got married.

To my surprise, he didn't quit preaching after all. They're still at that same church and that church is thriving. Having a former jailbird for a preacher and a preacher's wife who is a reformed gambler hasn't hurt them one iota. I don't know. Maybe it helps when people know you got problems, too.

Besides, them two people are doing a lot of good these days.

Long story short, instead of Lula Faye's lottery money going to an English estate that never existed, it got put into a foundation that funds church orphanages and medical clinics in places that need them awful bad. She and Roy live in the same house her and poor-stupid-Earl-bless-his-heart lived. Roy says after spending too many years in a small jail cell, it feels like a mansion to him. Lula Faye says that wherever Roy is feels like a mansion to her. Them two are just sick in love. I hope it lasts, and I think it might.

Everybody needs a love story to tuck away in their heart. Even a woman in her seventies. Captain Evan Stone is mine. Every now and then I think about Evan and how I got to sparkle at the captain's table and I am grateful to Lula Faye for making that happen.

Evan called me when I got home. He said not be surprised if he came knocking at my door some time. I told him that would be fine as long as there was no Mrs. Wilson tucked away someplace because I weren't that kind of woman.

He told me there was no Mrs. Wilson tucked away because she'd passed away a long time ago. Then he told me I could come back onto the boat anytime I wanted and travel down the river on the Mississippi Queen with him. It wouldn't cost me nothing. I told him that beautiful boat had kinda been ruined for me by what had happened on it when me and Lula Faye took our trip, but that he was welcome to come a'knocking at my door whenever he wanted to.

He said he'd be retiring after this season and would be taking me up on that.

In the meantime, the Mississippi Queen floats by South Shore every few weeks. Evan always calls to let me know when they'll be coming past. I pack a little picnic lunch and take me a mason jar of sweet tea and gather up my binoculars and then I go sit on the river bank and wait. Before long, there I am, and there he is in the pilot house a'looking back at me through his binoculars. The minute he sees me, he waves real big and then the calliope music starts. He says that music is just for me.

Like I said. Everyone needs a love story tucked away in their heart—and waving at that pretty boat with the handsome captain waving back at me is turning out to be mine.

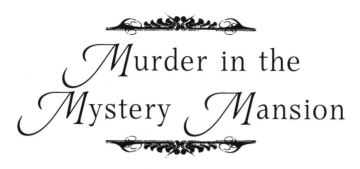

Murder in the Mystery Mansion

I've seen a lot of things in my life I wish I hadn't. My name is Doreen Sizemore and I'm seventy-two years old. Take my word for it. If you ever get to be my age you'll see things you'll wish you never saw neither. Things that make you want to just wash your eyes out with lye soap. Most of them things happened to me while I was trying to help out my kinfolk.

Being tender-hearted can get a body in a world of trouble.

I live in a little bitty river town called South Shore, Kentucky. It might just be a blip on the map to some people but it is paradise to me. I especially love my little town after going away on some of them trips where I was a'trying to help somebody out and got my fool self scared half to death stumbling over dead bodies.

Like I always say, nothing good ever comes from traveling. Bad things happen when I'm far away from home.

I was born and raised in Kentucky and proud of it. Up until the past couple years, the furthest I ever traveled was over the bridge to Portsmouth, Ohio where I had a job working at Selby Shoe Factory. I started in sewing shoes right after my graduation from Greenup High School. That's what us girls used to do around here. If you didn't get married and start having babies, you got a job at Selby's.

If you were fast at piecework--and I was--you could make a pretty decent wage. I used my pay check to help out Mama and Daddy with groceries and for things like buying football cleats for my little brother who weren't all that little in high school and had to have them cleats special ordered. Back then, I'd also buy a little lipstick and rouge from time to time.

My life in this river town has been a good one. At least for the most part it has been. The people tend to be pretty decent. I'm kin to some, friends with others, and I can tolerate the rest. We got us a high rate of unemployment just like everywhere else in the country right now, but the difference between us and the rest of the country is that we've been in a recession for so long we hardly notice it. We're good at rolling with the punches here in Appalachia. We have to be.

I remember seeing pictures awhile back in some magazine of a little kid with a dirty face a'playin' in the dirt. Underneath it they was asking for funds to help poor little Appalachian children. Them pictures were a puzzle to me. That child just looked like about half the other kids running around town needing a good face-washing before dinner. I couldn't see what the fuss was about, but then maybe they know something I don't.

Now where was I?

Oh yes.

People in South Shore, Kentucky know how to roll with the punches and help out a neighbor. It feels real safe when I'm here in my little house on the river where I belong.

So, after coming home with Lula Faye after that incident on the river boat that landed both of us in jail, I had it all figured out. I wouldn't leave town no more ever and nothing bad could happen to me. Nope. I'd stay in Kentucky where it was safe and I would mind my own business. That way I could depend on not getting mixed up in any more murders. Come heck or high water I weren't leaving town ever again and that was that.

I got me a nice life. I like being able to walk over to the beauty shop. I like being able to walk down to Foodland and get me some fresh pickle loaf every now and again and maybe a moon pie if I feel like it. Sometimes I splurge and get an RC cola. It goes real good with the home canned green beans I raise in my vegetable garden in the back yard. RC kinda cuts the bacon grease I use to season the green beans.

When I'm outside walking someplace or working in my garden, I talk to my neighbors if they're around and that gives me a good feeling. I have my social security check and my soaps on the television set every afternoon and a nice little church to go to come Sundays. And that's exactly the way I like it. Everything stays nice and safe as long as I mind my own business and stay where I belong right here in South Shore, Kentucky.

One of the best things about staying put in the town you were born and raised in is that you know where everybody fits and what their temperament is and who you can depend on and who it's good to steer clear of. For instance, there's the little couple next door. My cousin, Bobby Joe and his wife, Esther. She's got a brand new baby—her second one in two years. Her husband is not real work-brickle but he's young and strong and can be helpful in a pinch. It's good to have young muscle around when something needs to be moved or lifted and he's nearly always around.

Then there's old Mrs. Anthony who lives two doors down in that little bitty trailer that has all the rusty buckets of roses growing around it. I know I call myself old sometimes, but Charlotte Anthony is really old. She's a hundred and one and still hobbles around with a watering can talking to her roses every morning and evening. Them roses must like what she's a'saying because they grow awful good. Her daughter says if the roses ever start talking back to her mother they'll put her in a home, though. Her daughter used to be my high school teacher, so being around them two makes me feel like a young pup.

My neighbors directly behind me, the Bruce's, has a house that kinda hangs out over the the Ohio River. Since he retired from working at the A-plant over in Ohio, they become snowbirds who like to live in Florida all winter and come home during the summer. That's fine by me. When they're gone, if it ain't too cold, I sometimes sit a spell in one of them deck chairs they leave out and then I got me a nice comfortable place to watch the Ohio River roll on down to Cincinnati.

They don't mind me sitting back there on their porch. They like it. They even give me their phone number to call them in Florida if anything bad happens to the place while they're gone, and a key to get in if I need to check on something like a busted water pipe. That key is not a temptation to me. I know I could go in and snoop, but what's the point? Everybody's life is about the same as another's anyway. At least it is around here. A little more money here or there, maybe a little more booze, or a few more kids, but all in all we're mostly just hanging on trying to make sense of things and cause as little fuss as possible.

Three doors down are the Hutchins family. He's a Greenup County boy, born and raised. He got his wife someplace else though. I can't remember exactly where. I think it was some place exotic like Nashville. I've always liked Glen Hutchins. He worked his way up to principal at the elementary school and he and Samantha have two fine-looking girls. One's a senior at Greenup High and the other one is a freshman. Good girls, too.

Mrs. Hutchins, Samantha, is polite but she's never warmed up to me much. I hear she was trying to get a name as a country-western singer back when they first met. Then the oldest girl baby came and Glen got a job back here at home, and whenever I've tried to talk to her she always looks like she's either someplace else in her mind or wanting to be. I know I'm not the most interesting old woman on the planet, but I try not to outstay my welcome when people are busy.

They live in a house that Glen inherited from his grandma on his momma's side. It's a fussy sort of place. One of them Victorian-type houses with lots of porches and banisters and lace curtains in every window. I've read that some people call houses like that Painted Ladies—like some of the old people used to call women who made their living doing things with men that they shouldn't have been doing.

I can see why them kind of houses are called that. The Hutchins' place has that sort of personality, like there's been things happen behind closed doors that shouldn't have happened.

Which seems likely. Glen's great-granddaddy weren't exactly a church-going man. He made his money as a gambler on the old river boats. His name was Mack McMurphy and it was rumored that he built that Painted Lady house out of gambling money. Not honest gambling money, mind you. Mack McMurphy was rumored to be an expert at cheating.

According to stories my grandma told me, McMurphy's wife must have been a hard woman, too. Grandma said that Henrietta McMurphy ran a speakeasy in the cellar of that house at night during Prohibition. Then she'd turn around and serve tea and fancy little cakes to the neighborhood ladies in her formal parlor in the afternoon. I guess she thought it would make people less suspicious of the goings-on in the cellar.

People say that one of the builders told his wife there was

some hidden rooms and secret passageways in the place. He weren't supposed to tell, though, and he swore her to secrecy. But some people don't stay sworn. She told a friend, who told another friend, and then it was Katie-bar-the-door and everybody in town thought there was some secret rooms—but nobody ever saw nothing and the speculation died down about it. Glen always laughed if anybody brought it up and would say that he wished the rumor was true, but he'd been all over the place and never found nothing.

My grandma said that some of the local women told her that they sometimes got the feeling that somebody was peeking at them when they were in the parlor. It gave them the shivers, they said. But my grandma said she was in that house plenty of times and never got the shivers. She said she thought the builder was just trying to make himself look big in his wife's eyes and it got out of hand.

Anyway, Henrietta and Mack McMurphy's days were pretty full.

They had one child, a daughter named Elizabeth Ann. Like so many children do when they become teenagers, she rebelled. Problem was, her parents were into so many shady dealings, the only way she could truly rebel was to get religion, so she did. She met a traveling salesman by the name of Hutchins who stopped by the church one Sunday probably hoping his piety would earn him some sales.

He stopped traveling once Elizabeth Ann married him and moved him into the Victorian mansion her parent's ill-gotten gains had built. They started having Bible studies in the parlor and tried to talk Mack and Henrietta into joining them.

Mack and Henrietta were pretty elderly by then, but they decided that life weren't hardly worth living anymore with Elizabeth Ann trying to get them to come to Bible studies beneath their own roof, so them two old people bought their selves a little riverboat and took off one night when Henrietta was asleep. They left a note saying they were headed down to New Orleans and for her to leave them alone. I guess she did. I never heard anything different.

You'd think all that drama would've rubbed off on the people born there, but Glen's about as mild-mannered and boring as a man can be. I guess all the interesting part got used up by his ancestors. Elizabeth Ann must have squelched all the interesting right out of that family.

Even though it's been owned by Hutchins people for years, around here some people still call the place McMurphy's Mansion, although some started calling it Mystery Mansion because of the hidden rooms rumors. It ain't really no mansion, of course. At least not anymore. But back when Mack and Henrietta first built it, the thing was so big and pretentious for these parts, calling it a mansion pretty much fit.

Still, it's always been Glen's pride and joy and he spends a lot of time painting and scraping on it and keeping the yard tidy. Which, around here is seen as a little eccentric. South Shore ain't exactly a fussy kind of place. No one minds if there's a car or two up on blocks in a neighbor's yard, or if an extra washing machine sits a spell on a front porch, or even if someone takes it into their head to plant begonias in that washing machine. The old McMurphy Mansion kinda stands out in our neighborhood because it's so nice.

We had a nice, normal, quiet neighborhood until that Samantha Hutchins ran off with a truck driver, leaving poor old Glen and his girls all alone by their selves in that big old house.

"I never should have tried to tie her down to this place," Glen told me a few weeks later when I took him and the girls a banana cream pie so I could say how sorry I was. "It was like trying to capture a beautiful butterfly and keep it in a jar. Samantha was meant for better things."

Well, I'd heard about her trying to become a country western star and giving up her dream to have his babies, but from what I've seen, people tend to do about what they want to do. There's some honkytonks around here she could have sung in if she'd really wanted to. Honkytonks was good enough for Loretta Lynn when she was starting out, but I guess Samantha weren't no Loretta Lynn.

She was a looker, though, I'll give her that. I'm sure plenty of truck drivers would have been happy enough to have given her a ride. Wait a minute. I didn't mean that like it sounded. Offer her a ride in their trucks, I meant to say, although I'm not sure that sounds any better. Maybe I better go wash out my own mouth with soap and water right about now.

But anyway, after Samantha took off with the truck driver her daughters and husband didn't seem to hardly know what to do with their selves. It's hard on a family when there's no mother in the house. It was as though they were just waiting around for her to come back and tell them what to do.

Her daughters are pretty girls like their mama, but without her there to guide them they started dressing a little trashy which was something that Samantha never did. Glen just walked around looking lost and sad. It was like they was all playing a part in a bad soap opera--keeping up their end of the deal, until Samantha came back and they could start living their normal lives again.

The house didn't go to pot, though. Glen has always been good about keeping things clean and fixed up at his place. I guess it goes with the job of being a principle at a school in a small town. You have to keep up appearances no matter what. If anything, he made things a little more neat than usual, like he was keeping it especially nice for in case his wife came back.

It was enough to break my heart to watch that little family try to move on, and trust me, everyone most definitely did watch that family. It weren't every day that a local principal's wife took off with a truck driver.

If there's one thing that I've learned about human nature, it is that where there is no information, people will make it up. Somebody will give an opinion and a couple more people will repeat it and before long you're hearing an opinion stated as a fact. There were a lot of rumors and speculation flying around.

A few people suggested to Glen that he file a missing person's report with the police because there was no telling what that truck driver might have done with her. Glen shook his head and said that she'd made it pretty clear she weren't never coming back to him. One person asked him if he'd take her back if she wanted him to. Glen got all misty-eyed and said he'd take her back in a heart-beat no matter what she'd done because he still loved her so much.

The girls had been real involved in school before Samantha left. The oldest was a cheerleader and the younger one was in the marching band. People told me that Glen would go to the games and sit all by his lonesome watching his girls do their cheerleading and band-marching and it would be like he weren't hardly there. They said he just stared way off into the distance like he was wishing his wife would come back.

As the days went on, there were some single women at my church I overheard talking about how Glen weren't all that bad looking and why on earth would a woman walk out on a nice man with a good job and he did have that nice big house. I knew it weren't going to be long before the casseroles would start rolling in. I figured Glen was going to find himself up for grabs soon with or without having any divorce papers.

It got to the point I couldn't stand listening to the talk any longer. I baked me some brownies, put them on a nice blue-flowered plate that I'd picked up at the Dollar Store, covered it all in tin foil and walked down the road to pay Glen a visit. He invited me in, all nice and polite as usual. I couldn't help but notice that the house was clean as a whistle, just like he kept the outside.

Weren't nothing wrong with him keeping the place nice. Cleanliness is next to godliness and all that but it struck me as real sad that the man didn't have anything more to do with his extra time than clean his house. I mean, he had two teenage girls at home. I figured there should at least be a comb or a shoe lace out of place but there wasn't.

It made me sad to see that he still had the big picture of Samantha over the fireplace he'd put there years ago. It must have been taken when she was in her country-western mode and was still thinking she'd be a big star. She was wearing a fringed cowboy shirt and tight jeans and cowboy boots and was looking soulfully into the camera while holding a guitar. I have an idea she didn't know how to play the thing because her fingers looked real awkward on the strings.

You'd think that if a wife ran off with a truck driver the husband would be angry enough to take her silly-looking oversized picture off the wall, but that weren't Glen's way. He surely did love that woman.

It started me to wondering if that's why she left. Some women can only take so much worship before they lose their respect for a man. A woman thinking her husband can't draw a breath without her is a dangerous thing. In some women's minds it gives them the license to do whatever they want. A person has to have some self-respect or there are people who'll run right over you.

I figured Samantha would come home crying as soon as the truck driver dumped her. It weren't like she was no spring chicken anymore. Samantha had some years on her even if she was good-looking.

It probably sounds like I didn't like the woman all that much and that ain't true. She was nice enough. Even brought me some chicken soup once when she heard I'd been laid up with the bronchitis. I guess it was that country-music thing that got under my skin. She'd bring it up now and again as though she needed to remind herself that she was special. I couldn't see why she wasn't happy with just having the good luck of giving birth to two healthy girls and having a good man. Seems like some people always take the really important things for granted.

"You hear anything from Samantha?" I asked Glen, as I handed him the brownies. "It's been what, going on a month now?"

"Twenty-eight days," he said. "It's like I got a counter in my head clicking off the time. And no, I haven't heard a word. Do you want to sit down?"

"Sure." I knew he'd probably rather I'd leave him alone-- grief does that to people--but I took a seat anyway. Sometimes what people want ain't exactly what they need. I figured Glen needed to talk to someone and I've found that people tend to talk to me because they figure I don't count all that much anyways.

That front room was interesting. Old Mrs. Hutchins had always called it a parlor and only used it for company. She was one of them women who collected things and the parlor was stuffed with doilies and antique dolls and pretty china figurines. There was a flowered carpet on the floor and tassels on all the lamps. Truth be told, it was kind of a smothery room. It surprised me that the only thing Glen had changed over the years was hanging Samantha's picture over the mantel.

He offered me one of my own brownies and a napkin. Then

he brought out some coffee and I settled in for a good chat. I had some things to say to that man whether he wanted to hear them or not. After all, I'd known him since he was a boy and I figured I had the right.

"There's some women at our church starting to talk about how you ain't that bad-looking and they don't understand why a woman would up and run away from you like Samantha did," I said. "I'm thinking you might have a string of 'em lining up on your porch before long if you ain't careful. It happened to my uncle when his wife run off. Trust me—taking up with some other woman right now won't do your girls a bit of good."

"I'm not interested in other women." He had the grace to turn a little red in the face. "The only woman I'll ever love is Samantha."

"That's probably not true." I took a bite of brownie and chewed while I thought about his comment. My brownies are from a box, they ain't nothing special, but they're still pretty good. "I think you'll get over this someday and start to notice other women, but I think it might be best to wait until your youngest is graduated from high school before you start in with all that mess of dating."

"Seriously, Doreen," he said. "I'm quite sure I'll never be interested in another woman again as long as I live."

"Unless Samantha comes back."

"Yes, of course. Unless Samantha comes back. She was my soulmate."

Well, I always find that soulmate talk kind of gaggy. Especially when a man says it. That's the kind of thing women say. Not men. I also noticed he weren't eating any of the brownies. Instead, he just kept his head down while he busied himself weaving his fingers in and out with each other like he was trying to weave himself back together.

My problem was, being me, I kept thinking there must be a clue. Something he'd overlooked. Like one of them computer dating things that might lead him to know where she went and who she went with so he could go try to get her back. Then it struck me that men who talked about soulmates are probably not the kind of men likely to go get their wives back. At that point I didn't have a lot of hope for Glen.

"Did Samantha spend a lot of time on the computer?"

"What?" His head jerked up. The man had been a million miles away in his head. "Oh—I see what you're asking. No. She wasn't much one for computers. She left that up to the girls and me."

"So she didn't meet some other man on-line?" I was proud of myself for knowing the term.

"No," Glen said. "She just up and went off."

"Did she tell you she was leaving before or after she climbed into the truck?" I asked. "Were you there?"

He shook his head. "She left a note. I found it when I got home from work. It was lying on the ironing board."

"Oh." This was the first I'd heard of a note. "What did it say?"

"Just that she'd found someone else, a truck driver, and wouldn't be back."

"No word to the girls?" I asked. "No excuses for what she was doing?"

"Not really," he said.

"Do you still have the note?"

"I threw it away. I couldn't bear to look at it and I didn't want the girls to see it."

"Oh." I guess that made sense. The note had brought him a lot of pain. I suppose it would be normal to throw it away.

"Are you sure you shouldn't talk to the police?" I asked.

"Maybe they could at least go find her. Your girls need to hear from their mother."

He looked up at me with the most sorrowful eyes I've ever seen. "You think having the police make her contact us would make the girls feel any better?"

I shook my head. It wouldn't, of course. Them girls were going to have to live with the knowledge that their mother had abandoned them as well as their daddy. It ain't a good thing to have a mother abandon you for a truck driver, not a good thing at all. Although with some teenagers I've known I could certainly see why it would be tempting.

I couldn't come up with anything else to say and Glen didn't seem interested in keeping up his end of the conversation, so I left. I'm not sure what I wanted to discover, but there was nothing there. I walked back to my little house and sat for a while and stewed. Seemed to me if I was a husband, I'd be chasing that woman down and giving her a piece of my mind over what she was doing to me and them girls. But Glen just weren't the type I guess. Made me wonder what kind of principal he was. From the looks of things, maybe not a very good one.

Life is hard, plain and simple. It just is. People need to get themselves some gumption if they're going to get through their lives with any self-respect at all. I'd always known Glen was a nice man but I'd never suspected until now that having his wife leave would cause him to sit there in his house like a noodle.

It weren't long until them girls of his weren't only dressing trashy, but they were acting trashy, too. The oldest one got kicked off the cheerleading squad for picking a fight with another girl. The youngest one quit the band for no particular reason. Just walked off the field smack dab in the middle of a half-time show. At least that's the way I heard it down at the beauty shop.

"She was a good player, too," Holly said as she pulled the curlers out of my hair. It was a relief to get them curlers out of there. Holly rolls a really tight perm and I'm always glad to get it over with. One thing good about getting a perm though, is that you can learn a lot while you wait around for your hair to process.

"According to my daughter," Holly said, as she pulled the curler papers out, "The Hutchins girl said she was tired of practicing that stupid clarinet and now that her mom was gone, she was going to have some fun."

"Uh-oh," Edith said. "That don't sound good. Teenage girls having fun means we'll probably see another welfare baby showing up before long."

Edith works in housekeeping down at King's Daughters Hospital in Ashland. One glance at her poor legs and feet and it's easy to see why she never has anything good to say about anything or anybody. Edith's been through too much and has gotten a real negative attitude. She's also helping raise two grandbabies right now because there's no daddy in the picture. Edith definitely considers herself an expert on what happens when teenage girls are out having fun.

"It's Jerri Lynn, the oldest girl, that I'm worried about," Holly said. "She seems to be the one most tore up, picking fights with the other cheerleaders like that."

"Glen will have them girls running all over him before long," Betty said. "He's too nice of a man to try to keep two daughters out of trouble all by himself. He can't even make the kids at school behave is what I heard. One of his teachers says she don't bother sending a trouble-maker to the principal's office anymore because the kids know that nothing bad will happen to them. She says Glen tends to have a long talk with them and send them back with a piece of hard candy in their pocket. All the teachers are upset about it. It ain't much help when the principal is nicer than the teachers."

"I never cared much for Samantha," Holly said. "She always drove all the way to Huntington to get her hair done—like my beauty shop just wasn't good enough for her. Now that she's gone I keep wondering if we all should have been nicer to her or something."

We all sighed. The fact of Samantha taking off with that truck driver had blown a big hole in our little neighborhood and there weren't nothing that could be done about it except maybe try to keep an eye on the girls and help out when we could.

It was the beginning of September when Samantha left and it had already turned November when I had the occasion to talk privately with Jerri Lynn. I was sitting on the Bruce's back porch a'watching the boat traffic. We'd had a late fall and the colors of trees along the riverbank on the other side of the river were really something. I'd made me a late dinner of boiled potatoes, cottage cheese, and creamed peas with a little bit of green onion in them and I weren't thinking about anything much except how pretty the fall colors were and how good my stomach felt.

I didn't hear Glen and Samantha's oldest until she'd already sat down beside me on the old glider I was using.

"Well, hello there, Jerri Lynn," I said. "I didn't hear you sneaking up on me. Gonna have to get me some hearing aids I guess."

Truth be told, I was tickled she'd come to see me.

"I was taking a walk, Miss Doreen," she said. "And saw you here. I thought it might be nice to have someone to talk to. Momma always liked you. She said you had a lot of good sense."

Well, that was a revelation. I'd always thought Samantha was kind of stand offish with me. Never dreamed she'd ever bother to say something good about me to her daughters. I realized I was hearing a catch in Jerri Lynn's voice. I took a good look at her and saw that the girl had been crying her eyes out. She'd taken to wearing too much eye make-up since her mother had left and now it was messed up all around her eyes something terrible. The poor girl looked like a blonde raccoon sitting there beside me with her hanky all wadded up in her hand.

"Always glad to have some company," I said. "What's troubling you, girl?"

Instead of answering me directly, she pulled something out of her pocket and handed it to me like I was supposed to know what it was. The thing was slender and plastic and I had no idea what I was supposed to do with it. I looked at her, puzzled.

"It turned pink," she said.

Jerri Lynn started sobbing, and then I got it. I'd never seen a gadget like that up close before but I was pretty sure this was one of them home pregnancy kits they're always advertising on television, usually with the woman being all excited about it.

This poor girl weren't excited. She was devastated. I just hate it when Edith is right. I had hopes she'd be wrong this time and this girl wouldn't be doing nothing except getting ready for college next fall.

"You're having a baby?" I asked.

She nodded.

"And you're not happy about it?"

She shook her head vehemently.

"You going to keep it?"

She shrugged.

"Have you told your daddy yet?"

She shook her head, no.

"Ah."

I didn't know what to say after that, so I sat there looking out over the river, rocking gently on the glider with that seventeen-year-old bundled up in her coat beside me, blowing her nose from time to time.

I guess I did the right thing just keeping quiet because after a while I felt a hand creep into mine and we sat that way for a long time, just holding hands, thinking our thoughts. I'd been the old lady down the street for most of her life, and I guess just being with another person gave her some comfort.

"Did you ever have any kids?" she asked, after a while.

"No."

"Do you regret it?"

I had to think about that for a while. Not having children was a mixed bag for me. On one hand, it would've been nice to have had a son or daughter. On the other hand, from what I'd seen, children tended to break their parent's hearts pretty regularly.

I answered truthfully. "Sometimes."

"If you'd ever had kids, would you have walked away from them to take up with some man?"

"No." That was something I could answer truthfully. "If I'd ever had children, there's not a man in this world who could have made me leave them."

I was sorry the minute I said it. It sounded like I was criticizing her mother and I wasn't. It was just how I felt.

"Sometimes I wonder what I did wrong to make my mom want to leave and never come back," she said.

"You don't know that she's never coming back," I said. "She might. People change their minds."

"But she didn't even send me and my sister a note. I don't understand."

"I don't understand either, Jerri Lynn," I said. "I guess the only thing you can do is take good care of your own baby now that you're going to have one."

"Do you think Daddy will be mad?" She sounded like a five-year-old child who'd spilt some milk instead of a nearly-grown woman getting ready to give birth in a few months.

"I think your dad will be surprised, but he'll help you."

"Thank you." She gave me a quick, totally unexpected kiss on the cheek and then flew off, leaving me there on the glider with that stab in the gut that I get sometimes when I allow myself to wonder why some people get to have such sweet children and don't appreciate them. And them of us who would have cherished even one chick have to live our whole lives trying to convince ourselves that we didn't really want a child at all.

I did something the next day I hadn't done in a long, long time. I went to the Dollar Store and bought me some baby yarn and a crochet hook and set to making a little yellow afghan.

In the meantime, I was proud of Jerri Lynn in spite of the circumstances. The pregnancy kind of settled her down and made her serious. She studied hard while her belly grew. The younger sister, Maggie, seeing the fix her sister had found herself in, straightened up and got serious about her school work, too. She even took up the clarinet again.

Glen, however, just kept looking seedier and seedier. His hair went uncombed a lot, his overcoat developed a drooping hem and he didn't do nothing about it. When I tried to talk with him, he seemed preoccupied and distant. I began to wonder if the man might lose his job from sheer grief. Or maybe his mind. He even kinda drooped when he walked. The talk at church about him being a good-looking man with a good job who'd been abandoned by his wife died down. None of the single women brought any casseroles over that I know of. Jerri Lynn told me that she and her sister started teaching themselves how to cook off of YouTube...whatever that was.

There was a bond between me and Jerri Lynn from that night on the river bank when she showed me the results of her home pregnancy test. She started dropping by from time to time after school. Sometimes she'd just want to talk. Sometimes she'd show me a little outfit she'd bought. Sometimes she'd just sit beside me while I watched my soaps—not talking, not crying, just needing a little company from someone who didn't judge her for what she'd done.

The thing about being a washed up cheerleader was that there weren't a lot of her girlfriend relationships that lasted through the pregnancy. I never asked about the boyfriend. She never told me about him, neither. I got the impression he hadn't stuck around or else she hadn't wanted him to.

Christmas weren't much to write home about. I saw Glen putting up some lights around the house but he didn't bother to take them back down again afterward. That's not too unusual in our neck of the woods. Taking down Christmas lights tend to be more optional here than in other places, but in the past Glen had always taken them down the morning after New Year's.

My brother and sister-in-law in Texas sent me a scarf and gloves and I sent her a nice box of chocolates and him a fruitcake. My brother hates fruitcake, so that was fun.

Jerri Lynn graduated with honors in the spring. She told me she intended to take on-line college courses for a while until the baby was older. She wanted to be a pediatrician. I didn't think there was much chance of that happening but I'd been wrong about other things so I didn't discourage her none. This was one of them things I hoped I was wrong about.

It seemed to me like the bigger Jerri Lynn got around the middle, the skinnier her daddy got. Glen had been kind of a rounded-out man before Samantha left. Not really fat, but not muscular either. The kind of man who looked like he spent a lot of time eating good and sitting at a desk. The further she got in her pregnancy, the more cadaverous her daddy became.

It was early June when Jerri Lynn came to my door crying her eyes out again. Once she stopped crying long enough to talk, it turned out that her mama had finally called but it was while she and Maggie was out getting groceries. Her daddy had taken the call. He said her mama was traveling way out West someplace and told him again that she weren't coming home ever. She said she was having too good a time with the man she was traveling with. Told him she was tired of being a wife and mother and liked going new places. She'd used a pay phone so he couldn't call her back.

This upset Jerri Lynn so bad and she was sobbing so loud, I hardly knew what to do with her. She was so near term, I was scared she might accidentally start her labor right then and there. She just sat there on my old green couch and howled. I guess she'd finally had enough. The poor little thing had tried acting up, and her mama hadn't come home. She'd tried being a good girl and getting good grades and her mama hadn't come back. The whole time I think she was expecting Samantha to show up and get things back to normal again. This last phone call had taken that hope away. I know she was frustrated nearly to death that she hadn't been home to talk to her mama when she called.

I did the only thing I knew to do. I fixed her some tea and patted her hand and listened. But while I listened, I did a slow boil. I don't get mad very easily anymore. Seems the older you get, and the tireder you get, the less effort you want to expend getting upset. Just doesn't seem worth the bother. Over the years I've had about every emotion in the book. Some were enjoyable. Some weren't. Mainly they was all useless because a person still just has to go on doing what they gotta do anyway. No matter what their feelings are. Getting all up in arms about every little thing doesn't ever do a body any good.

But this time another woman's choices was just breaking my heart. I wished Samantha was there in front of me right then and there so I could give her a good talking to and ask her what in the world she was thinking of going off and leaving behind her two beautiful, good, daughters who loved her and needed her. Some people are almost too selfish to live and I decided that Samantha Hutchins was one of them people.

Tea and cookies can't heal heartbreak, but they gave that little pregnant girl something else to think about for a few minutes. She was hungry and they must have tasted good to her because she finished off the whole package before she went back home. When I walked her out onto the porch I could hear the mournful sound of her little sister practicing her clarinet. Jerri Lynn heard it, too.

"That's about all Maggie does these days," Jerri Lynn said. "I sometimes get awful sick of hearing it, but practicing makes her feel better. Thanks for the cookies, Miss Doreen. I'd better get back to my sister now. At least we have each other."

I watched as that girl squared her shoulders and walked back to her daddy's. I never wished for someone else's daughter to be my own before, but that girl was starting to get under my skin. She was a brave one that one was.

Right before June turned into July, we had us a brand new baby girl in our neighborhood. Prettiest little thing you ever saw.

I don't know if it was being abandoned by her mama that caused Jerri Lynn to be so focused on becoming a good mother, or if it was just part of who she was deep down. Maybe a little bit of both. All I know is that every day about one o'clock when the baby woke from her nap, Jerri Lynn took to walking down to my house with her little one so I could see some new marvel. Like watching her turn over, or sprout a new tooth. By the grace of God she was a good baby which made it a little easier on Jerri Lynn.

It made me feel good to see my little next-door-neighbor, Esther, also taking Jerri Lynn under her wing. My neighbor weren't the best mother in the world, but she was far from the worst, and Jerri Lynn needed a friend nearer her age than me. She'd pretty much lost the ones she had at school. Of course to hear her tell it, she'd dropped them. Didn't matter. It's hard to run around with girlfriends when you're the only one toting a diaper bag and a baby.

Glen perked up a little after the baby got here but he was still on a slow downward slide and neither me nor Jerri Lynn had a clue what to do about him. I'd never put much stock in somebody dying of a broken heart, but that Glen seemed like he just might. I never saw a man fall so low for so long. If he'd a' asked me I'd of told him he needed some of them anti-depressing pills. But he didn't ask me so I didn't say nothing. Still, I was afraid if Samantha did happen to get tired of her other boyfriend and come back, after one good look at Glen she might high-tail it out of here again.

I didn't even know Samantha had a sister until the girls' aunt came in from Wisconsin about the middle of July to see the baby. Turns out there was only a couple years between Samantha and her younger sister, Charlene, and they looked a lot alike. Jerri Lynn was so happy having her aunt there. She toted up that baby and brought Charlene down to meet me.

Charlene looked so much like Samantha it was startling. At first I thought Samantha had come home. Then I took a second look. Charlene had a little more sag in the hips and was a little less plump in the face. Still, she wore her straight brown hair long and swinging like Samantha always did and frankly, I thought she had a more genuine smile.

"Oh, shoot!" Jerri Lynn said after she'd introduced us. "Emma has dirtied her diaper again and I didn't bring anything with me. I'll be right back."

I noticed that Charlene didn't make a move at going back to the house with Jerri Lynn. I got the feeling she wanted to talk with me and I was right.

"Glen called and told me what happened back in September when my sister disappeared," she said. "I haven't heard a word from her. Do you have any ideas?"

"Ideas?"

"Jerri Lynn tells me that you've solved a few mysteries in the past."

"But them were murders," I said.

Charlene didn't say nothing. She just sat there looking at me like she thought I should say something more.

"I was just at the wrong place at the wrong time," I said. "I'm no detective."

Charlene still didn't say anything.

"Are you thinking your sister didn't run off with a truck driver after all?" I asked.

"I don't know what to think," Charlene said. "She hasn't called me. Not once in ten months. That's not like her."

"Maybe she thought you'd scold her," I said.

"Me?" Charlene laughed. "I'm on my fifth marriage and it's getting shaky. I've been in and out of rehab so many times I've lost count. Just got out two weeks ago. I'm hoping it takes this time. I'm the black sheep of our family. Samantha knows I don't have a leg to stand on if I gave her a hard time about leaving old Glen."

"And she ain't contacted you?"

"Not a word."

"Well, I been thinking," I said. "Me and the girls down at the beauty shop have been talking about what might have happened. Menopause can make a woman a little crazy and Samantha is about the right age. Edith says she started pitching perfectly good furniture out the door when she was going through the change. Betty says she started writing letters to an old boyfriend she hadn't even cared all that much about. Fortunately she got her good sense back before she mailed any of 'em. Do you think going through the change might be a possibility of why your sister lost her mind and took off?"

"Maybe, except it never mattered how bad I messed up or how long I was in rehab, Samantha always stayed in touch with me one way or another."

That worried me. A woman might leave her husband for another man and never look back, but there'd be no reason not call her sister.

"What are you thinking?" I asked.

"I don't know what to think. I sure don't want to get my nieces any more tore up than they already are. I know I'm an addict and always will be, but I love my sister. I have a feeling I need to try to find her."

Well, that set my old brain to churning which is never a good thing. It kept me up most of the night examining other possibilities. None of them possibilities made a lick of sense, though. Glen said she'd left with a truck driver and called back only once. Glen Hutchins might be falling apart from grief over his wife's abandonment but I'd never known him to be a liar.

I hated to get something started, but after that conversation with Charlene, I decided to go have a chat with our local sheriff. Ben's a good boy. The fact that his granddaddy ran a moonshine still didn't hurt him in the election as much as what most people might expect. If anything, it helped. We tend to feel a little bit protective of our moonshiners around here, especially since most of us are kin to one or two of 'em. Ben's mama was a Culp, and they're good people. She taught Ben right from wrong and I don't think the family moonshine still is running anymore. Of course I could be mistaken about that. Ben's granddaddy did have a good reputation for quality. Not that I ever sampled any. I'm a teetotaler born and raised, but I've heard rumors.

Anyway, I went to have a friendly chat with Ben.

"What if somebody disappeared and the spouse said they'd left with somebody else and no one ever heard from them again. Would that raise your suspicions?"

"You're talking about the Hutchins?"

I nodded.

"There's nothing to make me think it's anything more than what Glen's been saying," Ben said. "His wife got fed up with family life and decided to make a clean break of it. It happens."

"She just never struck me as the type," I said.

Ben clasped his hands behind his head, leaned back and stared out the window. "I was suspicious when I first heard, and I did a background check on both of them. Glen's squeaky clean but so is Samantha. No domestic disputes. Not so much as an overdue bill or a parking ticket. With the exception of their daughter getting pregnant, it's been the perfect family. There's no reason to think otherwise."

"I'm sorry I bothered you," I said, feeling a little silly. "It's just that the girls miss their mother. Glen says she called recently and is way out west. It's the only contact they've had with her and they've been upset ever since."

Ben nodded. "She's a grown woman. If she wants to gallivant all over the place with whoever she pleases, I can't exactly arrest her for it. There's nothing I can do. I'm sorry."

"I guess I'll have to leave it alone then."

"Miss Doreen?" he said, as I was leaving.

"Yes."

"If you see anything unusual, let me know. I'll pay attention to anything you got to say."

That made me feel a little better. "You're a good boy, Ben. You tell your mama I said hi."

"I surely will." He smiled. "You take care of yourself, now."

Ben is not a bad looking man, but he does have them ears that stick out too far just like his daddy and a lot of freckles. Makes it a little hard to take him seriously as a law officer, even though he's a good one.

So, life went on. The baby got two bottom teeth and was the cutest thing you ever saw when she grinned at you—and that baby grinned a lot. She didn't know things weren't right at home. As long as she had her mama to hold onto, plenty of warm milk in her belly, and dry diapers, all was right in her little world.

With summer, the sadness over Samantha's leaving seemed to lift a little bit. Our neighborhood sort of shrugged and turned its attention elsewhere. I got used to the rhythm of Jerri Lynn's daily visits, watching the baby grow, and sometimes when there was a little extra left out of my social security check, I'd buy a play-pretty for the baby.

Jerri Lynn grew into the role of taking over the running of the household. She learned herself how to cook and watched over her little sister like a mother hen. She fussed over her daddy and got him to spiff up a bit, too. Even the Christmas lights came down. In August, which didn't seem hardly worth the trouble to me.

One evening that fall while Glen was at a school meeting, Jerri Lynn called and asked if I had an extra pound of hamburger. She was trying to make spaghetti and hadn't realized she was out. Foodland was already closed and she didn't want to have to drive all the way across the river to Walmart to get some.

Well, I did happen to have a fresh pound of hamburger in the Frigidaire and since it was a nice evening I offered to bring it down to her so she wouldn't have to get the baby out.

I don't know about where you live, but in our part of Kentucky a lot of people tend to do their visiting through back doors instead of the front. I guess it just feels friendlier. So I didn't think nothing about it when Jerri Lynn motioned me through the back door into the kitchen, which meant walking through the screened-in back porch.

It was the kind of porch somebody probably once thought would make a nice sitting place if it had screens on it to keep the bugs out. But like a lot of porches around here these days, nobody sat out there anymore. If they wanted to sit, they went inside and the porch just ended up being a catch-all place for boots and coats and odds and ends. Some people kept their chest freezers on their porches, too, and I noticed that that's where Glen's family stored theirs.

"You don't have any room for a pound of hamburger in that big ole freezer out there?" I asked, kind of teasing-like, as I handed her the hamburger.

"Oh, there's probably all kinds of hamburger in that freezer out there," she said. "But daddy lost the key awhile back and we haven't been able to find it since. He says it'll turn up sooner or later."

Well, I weren't surprised to hear that. Glen had been walking around in such a fog he probably hardly remembered his name most of the time, let alone where he'd put a freezer key.

She told me to have a seat at the table while she worked on the spaghetti so I did. She was a' bustlin' around the kitchen like she was a grown woman instead of only seventeen. I think she was showing off just a little bit for me and I didn't mind admiring how competent she was becoming. The baby was off in the other room being watched over by Maggie. I figured Jerri Lynn wouldn't be in my life much longer. She was a cute little thing and some guy would probably snap her up before long, baby and all and she'd forget all about her friendship with old Doreen. It made me sad to think that—I'd gotten real attached to the girl and her baby—but that's just the way it is sometimes with young people.

Jerri Lynn put a tea kettle on and served some to me just like she was used to being the lady of the house. Then she finished up the spaghetti and filled three plates without even asking me if I wanted to stay. Like I was part of the family or something. It was real nice and homey. Her little sister brought the baby in and put her in the high chair and we had us a sort of spaghetti and tea party. Nothing is much cuter than watching a baby with only two bottom teeth trying to eat spaghetti.

Glen walked in and his face brightened at the sight of his daughters and grandbaby. He and me have always gotten along, so he didn't seem upset to find me there neither.

I walked home afterward feeling pretty good about things and thinking that maybe that little family was going to be all right after all. I was glad for the small part I'd had in what healing they'd had. I try to keep my nose out of people's business, but sometimes you can't help it. This time I was glad I got involved.

That night I slept like a baby until about four o'clock in the morning and then I had one of the worst nightmares of my life. I dreamed that Samantha was in trouble and was calling out to me. I could see her so well in my nightmare and could hear her voice so clearly that it made me sweat. She was just a'begging and a'begging me to help her.

The nightmare was so real that I woke up shaking and shivering and with my heart going ninety-miles an hour. I got up to get a drink of water, hoping I could finish getting myself out of the feeling of being in the middle of that nightmare. I just about fell down because my knees was so weak from the upset I'd had.

There weren't going to be any more sleep for me that night, so I started in on a project I'd been putting off a long time— cleaning out the pantry. By six a.m. I'd thrown out so many expired canned goods that I was ashamed I'd let it get to that state. I had seen that hoarders show when I was at my nieces down in Little Rock and she had cable TV. It give me shivers to see all them people who let things pile up around their ears. I was determined not to let that happen to me. I didn't want to end up on no TV program looking like a crazy lady.

So by around seven, I had eaten my breakfast, the nightmare had pretty much worn off, and I was feeling fairly good about things again.

I finally got the little afghan I'd been crocheting finished while I watched my stories that afternoon. My fingers ain't as nimble as they used to be. I was a little late with it, but better late than never, I always say. I wrapped it up all fluffy in some nice tissue paper and walked it down to the Hutchins. Nobody was at home, so I left it on top of the freezer on the back porch. I thought about what a nice surprise it would be for Jerri Lynn to find the present waiting for her when she got home.

Weren't long before she called to thank me. She'd taken the baby out for a checkup at the doctor's office and found the package when she got home. I went to bed that night feeling real good about myself. I figured that since I hadn't eaten a big plate of spaghetti before I went to bed this time, I was pretty sure I wouldn't have me any more bad dreams.

I was wrong. This time the nightmare was even more intense. Samantha was still calling for help. I was struggling to get to her, but I couldn't. It was so strange. When I woke up I couldn't figure out why this was happening now instead of all them months ago when her leaving was still fresh. All this time I'd known she was gone I'd been worrying over Glen and the girls and the baby. I'd never worried a whole lot about Samantha—except for wanting to smack her for leaving her family.

There are people who make claims to being psychic. I'm not one of them people. I've heard tell of parents who dreamed that their children was in trouble and then found out that they really were. I've even heard of spouses so close to each other that they could tell when one or the other had died clear around on the other side of the world, but I don't have that in me. Even if I did, why would Samantha try to contact me of all people? I weren't all that close to her.

It just didn't make sense.

The third night, I laid down in my bed kinda careful-like, half afraid of what kind of nightmare I might have this time. I didn't even make it to two o'clock before I had another bad dream. This time, Samantha was crying out that she was cold and needed the baby's afghan to cover herself.

That woke me straight up. I found out that I'd kicked all the covers off and was shivering again—which explained about the cold and the baby's afghan I suppose. I made myself some cocoa. Then I grabbed my Bible and tried to calm myself down by reading the Psalms. It helped some. It helped enough that I could start to think clearly again even if it was plumb in the middle of the night.

The thoughts that started coming weren't good ones, though. They weren't good at all. I had to rock and pray about them for a long time before I got some peace and could go back to bed. My sleep was uneasy because of what I knew I needed to do once the sun came up.

The next morning I watched as Glen left with the youngest

daughter riding beside him heading off to that band camp the girls had told me she was going to down in Lexington. That left only Jerri Lynn and the baby. I didn't want them around while I did what I had to do so I called Jerri Lynn and told her I needed me some Epsom salts and rubbing liniment for my sore back and would she mind too much driving over to Walmart and getting me some. I didn't lie. I did need me some Epsom salt and rubbing liniment. I was truly out of it, but I didn't need it so bad that she had to go right then.

Sweet thing that Jerri Lynn is, she agreed immediately even though it was going to mean dragging the baby out. She stopped by and I hobbled out onto the porch to give her the money—making sure I walked bent over so she wouldn't think I was faking it—which I wasn't. At least not entirely.

"Will you be all right here by yourself, Miss Doreen?" she asked.

"I'll be fine," I said. "I just need me a little sit-down in a bathtub of salts and some liniment. I appreciate you doing this for me."

"I'll be right back," she said. "I needed to pick up some diapers anyway."

With that she pulled on out to the highway and was gone. I figured I had about an hour before she came back.

I hurried up and got me a crow bar out of my daddy's old shed out back. I weren't happy about what I was going to do, but I knew it had to be me that did it. I weren't going to involve anyone else. If I was wrong, then it would just be me that was wrong. Nobody else would have to take any blame—not even Ben. Sometimes it pays to be an old lady. No one expects all that much out of you. If nothing else I'd pretend dementia had finally kicked in. Dementia is always good for an excuse when you need it.

Problem was, I was pretty certain I wouldn't need any excuses. I was too afraid I was right.

Here's the thing. A man raising two daughters on a principal's salary ain't likely to write off a freezer full of good meat. I knew that he'd bought a full side of beef right before Samantha left. He and one of my cousins had split a steer. Even in his mental fog, Glen had to eat and I figured that for most men, if there was only a little bitty lock between him and several hundred dollars' worth of Angus steaks he'd find a way to get to them, even if he had lost the key.

I was thinking it was a whole lot more likely that he'd thrown the key away or hid it—and that made me feel kinda sick to my stomach.

I felt a little conspicuous walking down the street with a crowbar in my hand, but nobody stopped me or asked me where I was going. I had one hour at the most, and I intended to use a lot less than that. I like my sleep. I was tired of having nightmares and this was the only way I knew I might get me my sleep back again.

Jerri Lynn hadn't locked the screen door on their back porch. I knew she wouldn't. Weren't anything there worth stealing. I was grateful the back porch faced the river instead of the road. It meant there was no neighbors watching when I popped the lid on that chest freezer.

It didn't take all that much effort. Not even for me.

The really big effort came in trying not to scream bloody murder when I saw what was a'layin' there on top of all that beef. I took one look, dropped the crow bar, threw my hand over my mouth, slammed the freezer door shut, and went as fast as my old legs would take me right back to my own house where I locked the door and stood inside, leaning against the door, trying to calm down enough to keep my heart from jumping plumb out of my chest.

As soon as I quit whimpering, I dialed Ben's number and told him what I'd seen and hoped never to have to see again. He came lickety-split over to my house.

When he knocked on my door, I managed to pull myself together and let him in.

"Are you sure?" he asked.

"Oh yeah," I said. "I might be old, but I can still tell the difference between a side of beef and a woman still in her nightie with her head bashed in."

"You stay here," he said.

He didn't have to tell me that twice. I weren't sure I'd ever stick my nose out of my house again. Not with these types of goings on in the neighborhood.

Weren't long before the police went to the school and arrested Glen Hutchins for the murder of his wife. I saw them drive him home in the squad car to talk to him about what they'd found in the freezer. Ben told me later that he'd never seen a grown man cry so hard. When they got him to the jail, they had to put him on suicide watch.

Turned out that most of his story was true. He and Samantha hadn't been getting along so good, although they'd been good at hiding it even from their girls. He was trying to be reasonable. She was wanting to go away and "find herself." He knew that was usually short-hand speak for "I think I can find someone better than you." He got scared he was going to lose her.

The girls were both having sleepovers with girlfriends that night. Samantha and Glen were free to fight as much and as loud as they wanted. Samantha was ready to march right out the door, nightgown and all. Glen was determined that she was going to listen to reason. They wrestled around in that overstuffed parlor in front of her picture. He shoved her. She tripped over a ceramic cat on the floor and fell backwards against one of them marble-topped tables and the woman never woke up again. When he realized she was dead and he might have been responsible for killing her, he panicked. The girls were due home in a few hours and there was blood on the floral carpet and splashed around on some of the furniture. He stashed Samantha away in the first place that came to mind, just temporarily, to give himself some time to wash away the blood, clean himself up, and think things through.

And that's what he'd been doing all this time—trying to think of a way out of this mess he'd gotten himself into. No matter how hard he thought, he couldn't come up with anything.

I said before that Glen was kind of a soft man. He might have gotten mad enough at Samantha to shove her, but he didn't have enough gumption to march down to the police station and own up to what he'd done. He said later at the trial that he knew it would probably cost him his job and he didn't want to lose it.

To the very end when they led him away to prison, he was still trying to make sure everyone liked him and didn't think he was a bad guy who had killed his wife on purpose. He kept saying it was all an accident and a misunderstanding. I'm sure it was. But really. What kind of a man sticks his wife in a freezer?

It was the most excitement South Shore had experienced in a long time, but it was the bad kind of excitement. The murder was interesting, but you felt bad thinking or talking about it. People were careful around the girls. We're all hoping it's the last excitement we'll have for a long while.

Bless that Ben's heart, he played down my part in the whole thing the best he could, but it still got out that I'd been the one who had put two and two together. Some people thought Samantha's spirit was calling out to me, but I don't buy that. If her spirit was going to call out to anyone's it would have been one of her daughters or her sister. As I said before, I ain't no psychic and she and me weren't close.

I know it was my subconscious trying to tell my fool self what I should have figured out long before—a woman might walk away from Glen, but she'd never walk away from her daughters without at least talking with them. I hadn't known Samantha well, but I did know her daughter's and it was a decent, caring woman who'd raised them two. Young mothers as loving as Jerri Lynn didn't learn how to love her baby all by herself. That girl had been nurtured.

It was also my subconscious or God or just common sense that made me figure out that the old chest freezer was the perfect place to store a dead body until a man could figure out what else to do with it.

It was no wonder Glen had gotten a little seedy-looking considering everything that must have been going around and around in his mind all that time. It must have been terrible for him knowing what he'd done and then trying, like some little boy, to cover up his mistake before anyone could find out.

It weren't easy on the girls. They loved their daddy, but they'd loved their mama more. It was hard for them to figure out how to act. Especially the youngest. That fall, there was a lot of mournful clarinet playing in our neighborhood and no one said a word about it. I hear she's got a music scholarship to Morehead State come fall, though. I guess there's a silver lining to everything—although that one is a little thin.

Jerri Lynn is working her way through the nursing program over at Shawnee State University in Portsmouth right now. She still talks of eventually going on to becoming a pediatrician, and I'm starting to think she has enough gumption to do it. That girl is awful determined. This ain't a bad step for her. A nurse can make good enough money to support a youngin' or two. Haven't seen any boys nosing around, though, which is hard to imagine as pretty as that girl is. I think maybe what happened to her mama has put her off men for a while. Someday somebody special might come along, though. In the meantime I'm proud of how she's doing. Proud as if she were my own. She still comes to see me, too.

Aunt Charlene came back to stay with the girls after her divorce. Both girls were still under age and needed an adult relative there so they could keep living in their home. Charlene seemed to be in a good patch as far as rehab, so that worked out pretty good. From what I can tell, she's still clean and sober. Sometimes I wonder who is raising who, though. Jerri Lynn is a lot more mature-acting than her aunt. I think it gives the girls comfort having her there, though. She does look a lot like their mama.

Got us a new principal down at the elementary school. I think it's working out a lot better. Glen seemed to have some trouble keeping his mind on his work.

As for me? I don't know. This was a bad one. It weren't just that I got myself involved in solving another murder. The thing that troubles me is that the murder was here at home. A person needs to feel safe where they live. Now my faith in my home has been shaken. I can't pretend that bad things only happen in other places anymore. I have to admit that there's plenty of bad anywhere you want to look, and sometimes it takes opening up other people's chest freezers to find it.

I figure a person has a choice in this life. You can see evil, or you can see good. I find it less stressful to see good as long as the evil don't get up in my face. When it does, I try to deal with it the best I can. That's all anybody can do.

Now, you'll have to excuse me. I just made me a fried bologna sandwich with a thick slab of ripe tomato straight out of my garden on it. I got my shoes off, an ice-cold can of

RC cola to wash it down with, and Days of Our Lives will be coming on any minute.

P.S. One of them good things I try to believe in happened to me a few months later. I was minding my own business when somebody came a'knocking on my door.

I about dropped my teeth when I saw who was standing there. Captain Evan Wilson from the Mississippi Queen had come a'looking for me just like he said he was gonna do some day. It was dead winter when he came and it turns out that they don't like for the boat to run in the middle of the winter months. It's a danger to the ship and besides that, most people don't want to cruise on the river in January anyway.

Evan ain't that shy boy I once knew back in summer camp and met again fifty years later when my cousin talked me into taking a cruise on that river boat. No, Evan ain't shy at all. He told me straight out that he'd deliberately come courting. He said I was the most interesting woman he'd ever met and he weren't about to let me get away from him a third time.

Ain't that something?

He's been a widower for a long time and it turns out he has a big family strung around all over the place. Four sons and two daughters and a dozen grandchildren at last count. He says he can't wait for me to meet them. He says they've been after him to find some nice woman and settle down.

It's early days yet. I ain't jumping into something right off the bat like Lula Faye did. But I'm having an awful good time getting to know this man.

I've talked it over with Jerri Lynn, and she tells me I need to "go for it." I think I just might take her advice. That girl has a good head on her shoulders.

Once while we was a'talking, I told Jerri Lynn all about them rumors of hidden rooms and secret tunnels. She asked Glen when she went to see him in prison and he didn't seem to know anything about them. So, level-headed girl that she is—she didn't go hunting around. Nope. She just asked a contractor to take a look and see if there was any evidence of it.

Turns out there was a tunnel that led to the river she's sure her great-grandma Henrietta used to secretly transport bootlegged whiskey up from the river back during Prohibition. She knows that was what it was used for because when they opened it up, there was a bunch of old whiskey bottles someone had left down there and forgotten about. Jerri Lynn found a collector who paid good money for the bottles and the story.

The contractor also found a secret room off the main bedroom on the second floor that Henrietta had evidently ended up using to store the fancy clothes she'd worn. Flapper-type dresses. Good ones. Totally out of style when Henrietta took off with Mack for New Orleans, but beaded originals worth a mint now. Some nice jewelry, too. Jerri Lynn is using what she gets out of the clothes and jewelry to help her with tuition and books.

I asked her if she was going to keep anything as a keepsake for the baby when she grows up. She said she thought getting an education so she can take good care of the baby might be a better use of the money. I agree.

Still, the other day she showed me one of Henrietta's dresses she's not planning on selling. At least not right away. It's all white with crystal beads. She tried it on for me and it drapes around that girl's body like it was made for her. Has a fancy-sounding label from Paris in it. Jerri Lynn said she thought it might do for a wedding gown someday so she thinks she'll keep it just in case.

I think "just in case" might come along before she realizes it. Ben was awful solicitous of her and the baby right after that awful time when I discovered her mother's body. I see him now regularly dropping by to check on her. Just a few minutes every week or so. A few words while he's standing there on the porch. Sometimes I see a teddy bear or other small gift in his hand. I know he's not the handsomest men in the world, but she could do a whole lot worse.

I always did think Ben had good sense and watching him these past months proves it. She's young, he's a good eight years older, so he's giving her time to grow up. She doesn't seem to mind his little visits one bit. I see him standing outside the door, talking to her, and I smile knowing what's probably coming in a couple years. I'm hoping I can see her put that pretty dress of her great-grandmother's to good use.

There's a saying that life begins at forty. I don't think I can go along with that. Forty weren't nothing special to me. For me, life didn't really take off until my seventy-first year when I pulled together what courage I had and stepped onto that train to go help my brother take care of my sister-in-law while she had the chemo. It was a hard thing to leave everything I'd ever known and go to Texas, but I did it. Now Evan says if I'll marry him we can travel the river together on a little houseboat he bought after he retired. He wants us to live part of the time on the river in his houseboat and part of the time here in my little house. I ain't said yes yet, but I'm surely studying hard on it. Evan says not to study too long because we got us a lot of living to do.

Jerri Lynn says if we get married she wants to make the wedding cake. The girl has been studying a YouTube video on cake decorating and she's getting real good at it. I guess maybe it wouldn't be too bad to travel outside of South Shore, Kentucky after all. Especially if I was on the river with Evan, and especially when I can always come back home for a spell. He says he's got a great-grandbaby fixing to come along pretty soon. A little boy. I bought me some fluffy blue yarn yesterday.

Imagine. Me. Who never had a child of my own getting a

chance to be grandmother to twelve and a great-grandmother, too.

I've changed my mind since Evan showed up. It does pay to travel outside of Kentucky every now and again. In fact, sometimes it pays off real good.

More books by Serena B. Miller

Non-Series Books:

Love Finds You in Sugarcreek, Ohio (Amish)
A Way of Escape

The Uncommon Grace Series (*Amish*):

An Uncommon Grace
Hidden Mercies
Fearless Hope

Michigan Northwoods Series (*Historical*):

The Measure of Katie Calloway
Under a Blackberry Moon
A Promise to Love

Non-Fiction Books:

More Than Happy:
*   The Wisdom of Amish Parenting*

Visit **SerenaBMiller.com** for more information and to sign up for Serena's newsletter or to connect with Serena.

37118577R00130

Made in the USA
Middletown, DE
20 November 2016